BABY DOCTOR

LEXIE MIERS

CHAPTER 1

TABITHA

As far as Tabitha was concerned the only thing magical about Christmas was the enjoyment of watching the snow fall while eating decadent food. And technically that could be done anytime during December through January.

Her baby sister's voice broke through her Christmas musings. "Hey, Tabitha! Can you pass me my water bottle, please?"

Tabitha glanced from her sister to the big pink plastic bottle she coveted and stifled the urge to laugh. She was only three feet but because her sister's stomach was *so* swollen with twins, she couldn't even get to her own feet without help these days, so Tabitha wasn't about to say 'no' to her simply request—especially when she needed to stay well hydrated for those two little munchkins in her belly.

"Drink up," she said as she grabbed the bottle and tossed it to her sister, who despite the chilly temperatures outside, sported rosy, red cheeks.

Samantha smiled gratefully and raised the bottle in a salute of thanks before she chugged back the water.

Tabitha's heart fluttered with happiness as she smiled at the picture her sister made. Samantha looked exhausted but radiant at the same time, reminding her of Mother Earth or Buddha. She hadn't decided which was more appropriate just yet. "Sam, seriously. How are you going to organize Christmas dinner for twenty people in your state? You know you were crazy for offering—actually, I take that back. You are absolutely *nuts* for insisting that you host Christmas dinner for the whole family this year."

Her sister laughed aloud, her big belly shuddering with each breath. "Yeah, I know. But it's the last time we'll be in Seattle for a *long* while, and I wanted to make it special."

"That doesn't mean you have to host it," Tabitha huffed. "It's so much work and you need to rest."

Samantha's husband had been offered a huge promotion by his employer and the pair of them had soon realized they'd be stupid not to jump at the opportunity. It would mean more money, more stability, and more sunshine! The only catch was, of course, that it meant a five-year commitment to a company in another state, a whole six-hour flight away.

Since she'd first found out Samantha was moving, Tabitha had been working extremely hard to ignore the twang of pain in her chest she experienced every time she thought about her sister leaving. They'd always been really close, so it was hard to imagine being apart. But she didn't want to make a big deal out of it and bring her sister's mood down. This would benefit Samantha and her family, and if she loved her, that's all that should matter.

Samantha sighed heavily. "Yeah, I know. I could have let you or one of the cousins take over, but I really wanted to do this, myself. And, you know, if I'm lucky, the twins will come a few weeks early, and they'll be here to celebrate Christmas with us! That would be the best Christmas gift, ever. The whole family would get to meet them, then."

Tabitha choked on her laugh. What a strange hope her sister was pinning her Christmas plans on. Most mothers-to-be wanted their babies to stay nice and snug in the womb for as long as possible; especially when it came to twins who were prone to come early, anyway! "Is that seriously what you want? You'd end up so sleep-deprived you won't be able to see straight, let alone cook, and we'll be having sweet potato casserole for dinner because you know that's all Mom's bringing this year."

After several decades of their mother hosting every single thanksgiving and Christmas event for their whole family, she'd given up the 'honor' to the next generation.

This was their very first year of doing it all, and Tabitha could already see that they were destined to fail.

"Don't be such a scrooge, Tabby. You know I'll be high on love and Christmas magic. You'll see!" Samantha grinned at her, then winced immediately after as she shifted in her chair.

Tabitha shook her head and grimaced as she stood up and collected the empty plates from the table. "Christmas magic, my ass," she quipped, taking care of the tidying up before her sister could.

Samantha scowled at her indignantly, as if she'd been robbed of the ability to prove just how capable she was fully preggers with twins.

but Tabitha didn't care one iota. She was the older sister and would damn well look after her baby sister as much as she wanted to. With a small smirk, she went about her business, cleaning up after her elephant-sized sister and washing the dishes from earlier in the morning.

Samantha's pregnancy had been a lot harder on her sister than she'd ever want to admit to, and Tabitha personally couldn't wait for those babies to make their grand entrance into the world, primarily so she'd get her lively, happy sister back.

On autopilot, Tabitha put away the milk that had been left out on the counter before noticing the twins' ultrasound pictures, magnetically stuck to the refrigerator. The smudges of black and white still looked so strange and alien to her.

A baby... two babies!

She sighed. Oh, how she wanted some of her own, but her baby sister had beat her to the punchline.

At thirty-one, her biological clock had begun doing some serious ticking. So loudly, in fact, she could feel the tangible tug of quiet jealousy on her ovaries every time her sister's husband brought home some new toy or trinket for his impending offspring. She shook her head at the thought of John, and it brought a smile to her face. He was such a big softie and she adored him for how much he loved her sister. They had a truly beautiful relationship.

The sound of heaving, huffing, and groaning in the family room reached Tabitha's ears and she hurried back to her sister. "What's wrong?" she asked, her brow furrowed.

"Toilet time," Samantha announced apologetically, holding her arms up for assistance.

Tabitha laughed as she reached out and pulled her sister to her feet, holding her steady. "And what do you do when no one's around to help you up?"

Samantha, now on her feet and looking twice as big as she had when she was sitting down, put both hands on her lower back and began waddling to the bathroom. "Oh, it's not a pretty sight," she called back. "And to be honest, most of the time I just make sure that I'm not sitting down. It's easier to clean a floor than a couch, you know?"

That was *not* as comforting a thought as her sister probably expected it to be. Tabitha sighed as she watched her sister disappear down the hallway. If she didn't work so many shifts at the hospital, she could be around more often to help. But with her mortgage as high as it was after her asshole ex-husband left her, she just couldn't afford to work any less or take time off.

A ripple of anger had her clenching her back teeth at the mere thought of her ex. He was such a narcissist. She'd been sucked in by his charming smile and false promises far too easily in hindsight. Tabitha was ashamed of herself, actually. She'd practically handed herself over on a silver platter, meanwhile he'd moved on to greener pastures, and hooked up with a wealthy ophthalmologist on the other side of the city.

Her job nursing the sick and injured had never been glamorous enough for him. And neither had she. In his eyes she wasn't pretty enough or skinny enough, she was just *never*... enough. So, when he'd followed his dick to some pretty blonde who fulfilled all his dreams of what he thought he deserved in life, she'd filed for divorce, taken out a loan to buy him out of the house, and had been working her butt off ever since to claim back what was left of her life.

"So, what are you making for Christmas?" Samantha asked. "You haven't told me yet, and I have to start organizing the menu," she said, as she waddled back into the room, one hand on her hip.

"Whatever you're missing, sis. I can do salads, turkey, a dessert or two? I'm easy." Plus, she'd do the decorating, dress the tree, and take care of all the clean-up before and after the event, if necessary. She'd attend to anything to keep her sister as relaxed as possible. Samantha's heart was huge, but her physical limitations were being exacerbated by the day.

"A salad, your broccoli-rice casserole, please, and a dessert would be great! I'm doing the turkey," Samantha said, happily stroking her belly in a soothing motion.

"Not a problem," Tabitha answered as she checked her watch and groaned at the time.

Late as always.

"Damn it. I better go. My shift starts in half an hour and I'm already pushing it." She leaned down and kissed her sister on the cheek goodbye.

Samantha kissed her in return. "Go, go! I have a doctor's appointment in a few hours, so I'd better start getting ready for that. Thank you so much for coming by. I appreciate the company and the help."

Tabitha turned to walk away but stopped mid-step and walked back to rub her sister's swollen belly gently.

Thirty-two weeks down, hopefully not more than four to go!

"You two need to come out soon, so I can meet you," she said with a grin.

There was a distinct shift and tug of flesh beneath her hands as her niece or nephew kicked out at her.

"I hope they do too, then you'll get to see them before we leave," added Samantha. "They could use Aunty cuddles before we go."

Yep. Ouch. There's that horrible heart tug again...

"You better have a spare bedroom for me to crash in, Sam," Tabitha called out as she made her way toward the front door. "You know I'll be there every other weekend, as frequently as I'm able, whenever I have a few days off in a row."

"I'll be counting on it. And I can't wait for you to come visit." Her sister waved her off with a smile.

Tabitha pulled on her coat and rushed out the door to her car, the cold air made her skin tingle, reminding her it had been a solid choice to wrap herself up in five layers of clothing.

They'd always been super close, Sam and herself. Born only

eighteen months apart, they'd been inseparable during their child-hood, worst enemies throughout their teenage years, and now they were each other's best friend, again.

Tabitha knew that she couldn't continue to ignore the fact that her rock was leaving her—her only sister—the woman who'd given up every weekend for months, coaxing her through the rigors of a painful divorce, and even worse, true heartbreak.

Her sister now had the opportunity to travel, see new and exciting things, and support her wonderful husband in the process. Not to mention the salary he'd be on meant they could pay off the house they'd bought, and Sam could stay at home with the twins for years, if she chose to. It would be ideal for their instant little family. Her sister had absolutely made the right decision in marrying John Tennyson. She'd been lucky to find someone so devoted, down-to-Earth, and loving.

Meanwhile, yhere had been times when Tabitha had been ready to write off the entire male race as worthless. But then Sam would present her husband as a sterling example, and Tabitha's case would fall to shit in a heartbeat. The simple fact of the matter was that some men were assholes and some were not. And the same could certainly be said for women.

Tabitha turned over her ignition and listened to her old car fight the cold and try to start. It stuttered a few times but got there in the end. A smile lifted her lips. "Old faithful."

With a four-bedroom home to look after and a mortgage that two people would genuinely struggle to pay for, a new car was a distant dream for her. But she hadn't lost faith, not quite yet, that the man she was meant to have children with was still out there... somewhere. Hopefully, wherever he might be, he was thinking the exact same thing.

CHAPTER 2

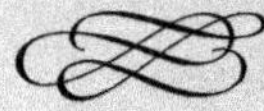

NOAH

r. Noah O'Grady was laser focused on the task in front of him. Bringing new life into the world was something he considered both a duty and an honor. "I can see the head, Karina, you're doing great. Just one more big push and your baby will be here."

His patient's sweat covered brow creased even more as she dredged up the last of her strength and with an almighty effort, heaved her tired body over the finish line.

The baby's head crowned, and their shoulders turned beautifully. Then in a rush that never ceased to surprise and amaze him, the baby slipped free of their mother's body and in the next heartbeat Noah knew what they were and caught her with both hands. He performed a quick check of her vitals and color, both were satisfactory and well within normal range.

The baby cried with a healthy enthusiasm, still covered in white vernix and fresh blood.

Just Perfect.

"What is it?" the mother asked, trying to peer over the white cloth they'd draped over her knees.

Noah wrapped the baby in a thin muslin blanket, then waited sixty seconds before he snipped and tied off the umbilical cord. Recent studies showed that even the shortest delay in cord clamping would ensure the newborn baby received a sufficient amount of its blood volume from the placenta, ensuring a better and more robust start to life. This was the second girl for his shift. He'd delivered three boys yesterday.

"You have a beautiful, healthy baby girl," he announced as he laid the baby in her mother's arms and accepted a stiff handshake from the father, whose eyes were understandably filled with tears.

The parents cooed over their newborn miracle and it was a sight that never grew old. That instant joy and love that filled a room was something else.

Noah washed up and instructed one of the interns to handle the post birth care. It was good hands-on experience for them, and simple enough that there'd be no concerns about their ability to fulfil the tasks. "Congratulations, you two," said, turning back to the proud parents. "I've got to head over to my office, but I'll be back a little later to check on how everyone's doing."

He had a mother expecting twins in his office at the other end of the obstetrical unit and a full book all day—as he did every day.

"Thank you so much Dr. O'Grady!" the mother chimed, positively beaming from ear to ear despite the physical toll a delivery took on a woman's body.

He smiled and nodded at the new parents and opened the

hospital room door. "You're very welcome, Karina, James. Congratulations, again, on your little bundle of joy."

"Mrs. Tennyson is waiting for you Dr. O'Grady," said a nurse as she handed him a file and accompanied him down the hallway to the entrance of the medical office suites.

"How late am I running today?" he asked with a lop-sided smile.

"Oh, only an hour or so."

He chuckled at her response and moved back into his office, pulling off his scrub top and replacing it with a clean one. That was the nature of birth and deliveries. They worked on their own clock, and you just had to roll with the punches as best you could, and usually under a lot of pressure. Grabbing his lab coat, he headed for the exam room across the hall.

"I'm so sorry about the delay, Mrs. Tennyson, but I had a baby girl who could just not wait to join us Earthside." A cynical thought crossed his mind as he glanced at his watch. He should probably schedule more C-sections like so many of his other colleagues. They kept their deliveries locked in for the weekends and their office hours during the week were uninterrupted. It was so much more efficient than the way he did it.

Yet, he just couldn't bring himself to recommend surgeries to women who were capable and willing to deliver naturally. It seemed ingenuous to convince an expectant mother to opt for surgery unless she had her heart set on it. And he'd certainly couldn't live with himself if he took a mother's choice away from her for his own convenience. He felt that went against the Hippocratic Oath. Birth was one of those things Noah firmly believed should happen in its own time where possible.

"Oh, not a problem, Dr. O'Grady. Babies will do as babies do, and you know I'd wait all day to see you." The heavily pregnant woman gave him her trademark sunny smile and he was yet again reminded of why he was always running late.

It was because he chose to support his patients in their personal birth plans, and that would forever mean he'd be over-booked and running from hospital to office like a dog chasing its tail. But ultimately, it didn't matter. It's what his patients wanted, and it was what they came specifically to him for and paid for with their hard-earned money. And it was the care he gave that he prized above all other things. He took great pride in his work, and he always would.

Noah walked into his room and sat down in his mercifully comfortable leather chair. It did feel good to take a load off his feet for a little while, though, he had to admit. "And how are you feeling, today, Samantha?"

The woman sitting opposite him gave him a shaky smile. "Oh, I'm very well. As big as a house, as you can plainly see, but overall, I'm very well, thank you."

When her grin didn't fade, he probed further. "All right, well, what can I help you with today, then?"

She rubbed her belly round and round, too quickly to be soothing. She was clearly feeling some typical first time-mom anxiety. "I guess I'm just a little concerned about how big I'm getting."

He frowned and took a calming breath. "Why, has your husband said something?" He loathed men who criticized their wives for the weight they put on during their pregnancies. In the past, he'd been known to take them into the corridor and give them as stern a dressing down as he dared.

It was hard enough for women to balance everything a woman had to do in an already demanding world, without having to deal with a man who had no idea what she was going through and dared to make snide or hurtful comments about their changing bodies. It genuinely frustrated him to tears.

"Oh, no, no! John is more than wonderful. He's so supportive. It's actually... me."

That seemed like a truthful answer, although he notated an

upside-down star on her private file for his future observations. "Samantha, most women lose their baby weight in the first twelve months after the baby is born, so there's nothing to worry about. Especially if you breast feed. Babies, especially twins, need more calories to thrive than you can imagine."

She shook her head. "Oh... no. Honestly, it's not that. My husband would love me even if I was fifty pounds heavier or lighter. And I don't really care about my clothes or anything like that..."

That's different.

He was fresh out of ideas as to why she could be concerned then. "Then what is it?"

She chewed on her lower lip and shifted in her chair. "I'm just *so* uncomfortable. I seriously can't get up off my couch by myself And I can barely waddle to the toilet some days. There is no way I can do my own laundry or clean. I'm totally useless and I really hate it. Especially with Christmas coming! I'll never be able to cook or organize the day how I'd like to for the family."

Noah sat back in his chair and laced his fingers in thought. December was already here.

Damn.

Part of his brain had somehow managed to forget just how far into the year they were. Women did this to him every year. No one wanted to give birth on Christmas Day, and they often wanted to manipulate their due dates to avoid it entirely. He checked his paperwork with a grimace. "Your babies aren't due until the seventh of January, although very few twin pregnancies make it further than thirty-eight weeks."

Which would land her right on Christmas Day.

Now, he understood her concern. "Okay, Samantha. Look, you came to me because you said you wanted as natural a birth as possible, so I feel it's my duty to tell you that if you're asking for an induction, your chances of achieving a natural birth are significantly reduced."

Samantha frowned.

"Which, of course, is still totally acceptable. As a twin pregnancy, and therefore a higher risk pregnancy, we could book you in for a C-section any time after thirty-six weeks. The babies would be small, but they *would* be healthy."

Her face scrunched up. "Would they need to stay in the intensive care unit at thirty-six weeks?" she asked.

He considered the last few cases he'd had before answering. "About half the time I find they need to stay for a few days, just to gather their strength, but not usually much longer than that if all goes well. However, every case is different. Twins present a unique set of potential quandaries that singletons don't, I'm afraid."

She hugged her belly tighter. "I really don't want to be induced, and I don't want a C-section, either. But I'm not sure how much longer I can stay pregnant like this. I feel like a whale. I can't sleep, I'm in pain, constantly, and I'm struggling to do everything at home. And Christmas is stressing me out to no end."

Noah relaxed in his chair and took a breath. Samantha needed someone to take the pressure off her, and if no one in her family had done it already, then he'd happily do so.

"Well, you have to realize, I think, that Christmas might need to be a smaller affair this year than you'd necessarily hoped for, Samantha. Here are your options. If the babies come on time in January, which is unlikely, you'll be so big by December twenty-fifth that you won't be able to do Christmas as you would normally, anyway. If we induce you early, let's say in two weeks' time, the likelihood of a C-section is very high, *and* if we do a C-section, you won't be lifting or driving for at least six weeks. So, given the circumstances, I think you need to forget about Christmas, and focus on your own health and that of your babies."

Tears slipped down the young mother's cheeks upon hearing his ultimatum.

Noah pushed the tissue box across his desk. "I don't mean to upset you, Samantha, but my primary concern as your doctor is your health, both mental and physical. I will support you in any way that I can, but I think we need to work around your body and your beautiful babies, not December twenty-fifth."

"Yes, Doctor." She hiccupped as she wiped away the tears rolling down her face.

Noah stood up and offered her his hand. "Now, let's get you on the table and check out how these babies are doing." He helped his patient to get comfortable on his medical bed and rolled the sonogram machine over that would project the babies' heartbeats into the room. Hearing the music of their little hearts beating would reassure her that her children were the most important things in the world and that's what she needed to prioritize.

Not Christmas day.

Samantha began to smile, her tears drying as she laughed when her babies moved beneath his hands.

Turning his attention to the monitor, he focused on the job at hand, stifling the sigh that rose in his throat. The hardest part of his day had presented itself as he realized the Christmas craziness had begun and his usually packed schedule was about to get a whole lot worse.

CHAPTER 3

TABITHA

A message from Samantha came through while Tabitha was working, and she punched in the return call as soon she was off the clock. The moment that Sam picked up, Tabitha jumped straight in. "Are you okay? Is there anything wrong?" she asked, butterflies of anxiety fluttering haphazardly in her stomach.

Her sister's happy laugh sounded at the end of the line. "No, nothing's wrong! Honestly, relax," she assured her.

Hearing no trace of a lie, Tabitha did, leaning back against her locker in the nurses' room. "Oh, good, I'm glad. So, what's up then?"

Her sister didn't usually message her to say, "call me when you're finished work." Yet she had and here she was. "Um... I think you were right," Sam admitted with a mournful sigh.

Tabitha chuckled. "Um, about what, specifically?" Because there were literally way too many things to which Samantha could be referring to. As her older sister, Tabitha had offered her a ton of advice, despite not being the pregnant one. She'd worked in hospitals long enough to know a thing or two about maternal health, pregnancy welfare, and birth, as well as most things that came after.

"About Christmas." She huffed. "It's too much work for me to organize the whole day at my house. I'm barely coping as it is. So, I was wondering if..."

Tabitha jumped in, unable to hide the excitement and relief from her voice. "If I'd do it at mine? Absolutely, sis! Not a problem at all. I *did* tell you that you needed to rest up and focus on yourself and the babies," I added. Though she'd never reveal as much, it was kind of a major problem. She had no excess finance with which to splurge on decorations or extra food, but she had a credit card she could use in emergencies... and saving her sister from a physical and mental breakdown sounded like an emergency.

"Oh, thank you so much, Tabby. I really appreciate it. I don't know what I was thinking!" Her sister sounded instantly much more relaxed and a happy sigh floated through the phone.

But Tabitha was curious. Afterall, Samantha had been so dead set on doing Christmas herself, only just this morning. "So, can I ask... because, you know, curiosity killed the cat... what was it that changed your mind?"

"Oh," she said airily. "It was my doctor. He didn't like me being as stressed about Christmas and the timing of the babies' delivery, among other things. He told me to just focus on the twins and forget about everything else. So, it's very possible I'll be going into labor on Christmas day, but if you can deal with that, then we're all good."

Tabitha could have almost burst out laughing, but relief flowed through her like cleansing rain.

She finally listens when the same words come from a doctor? At least she's taking it on board, finally.

"Of course, I can deal with that!" she answered. "Really, I'm so happy right now, Sam, because you know he's right. Your health and that of your babies' is all that matters now. Besides, you know me, I'd be more than happy to skip Christmas all together this year."

"Tabitha!" Sam chastised.

"Yeah, I know." Tabitha rolled her eyes. She'd been just about ready to give up on life completely when her ex had left her, and Sam had been there to scrape her off the proverbial floor. It seemed one good turn deserved another. She knew how important these family events were to her sister, so she would come through for her no matter how she personally felt or what it took to pull off. "I'll have to thank this doctor of yours personally for bringing you to your senses."

"Well... actually. You might be able to do just that! It's getting harder and harder for me to drive safely given my belly, and with John working so much, it's going to become a problem. So, if you wouldn't mind, I'd love a lift to my appointment next week."

Tabitha smiled. "No problem. Just shoot me the details and I'll make sure I free up the time if I need to." She'd covered a bunch of shifts at work in recent times and was sure she could pull in a favor if necessary. She was certainly owed one or ten!

"I will. Oh, and by the way, I gave John your bank details and he transferred five hundred dollars to help cover the Christmas decorations, food, and alcohol, and everything. If you need more, can you let me know?"

Already?

She'd only just said yes! "No!" she protested. "You can't do that. If I'm throwing Christmas, I'll get all that stuff."

"You'll have to buy it all as it is, sis. It's the least we can do. I'm just sorry I haven't been able to do any of the shopping already."

"But..." Tabitha began again.

"Tabby, stop. Honestly, you're going to have to do all the cleaning, the setup, the cooking. The very least we can do is contribute toward the costs, and thanks to John's new job, we have the money. So, please don't stress or argue, okay? At least this way I feel like I've helped."

Tabitha blew out a heavy sigh. That was logic she found hard to refute. Even with the money, she'd still have to do a hell of a lot of work, and if nothing else, they were being super generous because they were the best people ever. "Okay. But no Christmas presents this year, right?"

"Yeah, of course," Sam agreed far too quickly for Little Miss Loves the Holidays.

"Sam..."

What's the bet she's already got everyone's gifts?

"Hey, sorry, but I need to go, Tabby. I'll see you at my house over the weekend?"

"Yeah, of course. And don't forget to send me those details for your appointment next week," Tabitha reminded her.

"Will do. Thank you. Bye for now!"

CHAPTER 4

NOAH

One week later...

A knock on his office door woke Noah out of his doze.

Sugar.

He cleared his throat and sat up straight at his desk. "Come in."

His receptionist stuck her head in with a smile. "Your next appointment is here, Doctor. Can I get you anything?"

A caffeine IV?

"Yes, coffee, please. Thanks, Cheryl."

Cheryl opened the door wide and ushered in his next patient before she went off to fetch his legal stimulant.

He'd had a rough couple of days and nights, and sleep had been very thin on the ground. "Samantha, please have a seat," he said, gesturing to the seats opposite him.

His patient waddled in a hand on her hip for balance as she offered him a grin.

He suppressed a chuckle. He loved when expectant mothers reached this stage of their pregnancies. Pregnancy might be beautiful and natural, and often referred to as a miracle, but at times like these? It was just adorable. Samantha's newly adjusted gait indicated that one of her twin's heads had descended into her pelvis and she looked like a big mama duck.

A very positive development.

"Oh, hi, Dr. O'Grady. My sister's here with me today, do you mind if she comes in too?"

"Of course, not," he answered, waving his hand in a dismissive gesture, giving his go-ahead for her to bring in whomever she wanted. A support person and advocate were always encouraged in his offices.

A woman walked through the door and smiled at him, the beauty of her face striking him low in the gut like a punch, almost winding him.

"Tabitha, this is Dr. O'Grady," his patient said, introducing him.

Tabitha, the blonde-haired angel stepped up to his desk and extended her hand in greeting. "It's so nice to meet you, Doctor. I've heard only good things."

"Noah... please," he managed to say as he stood up and shook her hand, his mouth running dry as most of the blood in his body pumped south. Samantha's sister was beautiful in all the ways he loved most in a woman. She had lovely full lips, a contagiously happy smile, and bright, warm eyes. Not to mention her perfect skin made him want to run his hands all over her and luxuriate in its firm softness.

"Oh, thank you. Noah." She gently pulled her hand away and helped her sister settle in a chair, her gaze dropping away as though embarrassed or shy.

They all sat down, and he took the cup of coffee Cheryl brought in for him, focusing on lifting the cup to his lips and having a long drink to steady his nerves. It had been way too long since his last intimate affair, obviously. He could barely concentrate with a beautiful woman within speaking distance.

"Excuse me while I just get my caffeine hit," he apologized.

"Long shift, Doctor?" Tabitha asked, in that particularly professional way that all his staff spoke to him.

He turned to her, despite his natural instincts warning him that prolonged staring could prove dangerous for him. "You're a nurse?"

She laughed in a short, shocked way, her cheeks instantly coloring with a pretty rose blush. "How did you pick up on that?"

God, she's beautiful. Those eyes...

"Ah... the way you said 'Doctor,' actually. Which hospital do you work in?"

"St. John of God."

"That's a lovely little hospital." St. John of God had very demanding staff requirements which would mean Tabitha would need to be classified within the top ten percent in both efficiency and professionalism. No doubt she was in high demand. As beautiful as she was, he could see the soft shadows under her eyes that belied her fatigue. When you lived the medical life, not even the best cosmetics could hide the constant and ongoing exhaustion that came with being on call and filling in shifts without reprieve.

"Yes, it is, and the staff are lovely." She smiled and he could see she was telling the truth. Maybe she enjoyed surrounding herself with exacting people?

"And what's your specialty?"

"I work in the E.R most of the time, but I float."

Well, that confirmed it, then. She was more than a hard worker. Tabitha would have to be brilliant to juggle that workload successfully and the demands that came with it, and he respected that. With a concerted effort he tried to keep his mind on the appointment he *should* be having with his patient, but he couldn't stop looking at the curve of Tabitha's cheek, and the attractive waves in her long hair.

She also emanated a natural sense of warmth that he found extremely attractive.

I bet she has an incredible bedside manner. Her patients must love her.

Too many women often suffocated that precious warmth with a modern, snarky attitude that grated on him. He didn't think it was necessary that a woman be a bitch to present as strong.

Someone cleared their throat and he looked across to Samantha, who was glancing pointedly between her sister and himself with a "cat that ate the canary" smile.

He slid back into his seat and focused on his patient, and not her beautiful sister though it almost pained his professionalism to do so. "And how are you today, Samantha?" he asked. "You're looking happier than you did at last week's appointment."

"I'm much better, Doctor, thank you. I'm still uncomfortable, but I took your advice and have palmed off all my Christmas responsibilities so that I'm not going to stress about times or dates. I'll just wait until my babies are ready to enter the world."

A smile kicked up the ends of his lips upon hearing her relaxed declaration. "I'm very glad to hear that. I've got you booked in for a routine ultrasound, just to check on your babies' growth and position. Would you like to do it now?"

"Oh, yes, please!"

Tabitha jumped instantly to her feet to assist Samantha in rising from her chair.

His patient lumbered up on the table and pulled up her flowing black maternity top to reveal her large, swollen belly.

"And you still believe a natural birth is possible, Doctor?" Tabitha asked, stepping closer.

Noah once again struggled to focus. He picked up the lubricant bottle and applied the gel to the end of the ultrasound wand. "Yes, I do. I have great faith in the natural method of childbirth."

Tabitha's mouth quirked up strangely. "Then you would be one of the only physicians I know who does."

He shrugged. He'd trained under an obstetrician that the other professionals referred to as "Lionel Vaginal" because he was known for his love of and advocating for natural births. Whether it was breech, posterior, footling, or twins, he'd delivered them all. Noah had an immense passion and respect for the innate intelligence of the man whose body hadn't given out recently after his long years in obstetrics. He'd believed adamantly in the power of the female body, and Noah had adopted those same beliefs himself, in his own practice.

"Our bodies are a thousand times smarter than our conscious brain. Innate intelligence is largely un-measured in the field, and pure magic as far as I'm concerned. Of course, I would never allow your sister to risk her life, or those of her babies. I'm here and prepared with a surgical room if need be."

The smile Tabitha gave him in response lifted his heart up and out of the dusty coffin it had been slumbering in for far too long. Then Tabitha turned her attention toward the screen and rested a comforting hand on her sister's knee.

Time to get back to work.

Noah focused on the job in front of him. The screen lit up with black and white grainy images and he moved the scope around Samantha's belly to determine the position of her twins.

"Wonderful news!" he said. "One baby is moving into the engagement position, head down, and the other is head up, under your ribs."

Samantha laughed as her gaze followed his movements on the screen. "Yeah, I know. I can feel him or her. They've been knocking the breath out of me somedays."

Tabitha moved away without a word and sat back in the chair by his desk.

"Are you all right?" Noah asked her, though she didn't look visibly upset.

Tabitha's gaze met with his.

A fission of animal awareness shot through him. He wanted to groan aloud. This was so amazingly inconvenient. He was always a consummate professional, yet she was eroding the very foundations upon which he stood. Why couldn't he have met her at a restaurant or bar one night?

Because you do nothing but work.

"Oh, yes, of course. Please don't mind me. I just don't want to see what gender they are, and I don't trust myself not to look."

"No! I don't want *you* knowing if I don't!" Samantha cried like a child about to have her birthday surprise ruined.

Tabitha rolled her eyes in a way that only a sibling would. "I know, Sam! That's why I'm all the way over here."

Noah chuckled. He couldn't help himself. He was used to being the comedic relief in his consulting rooms, lessening the tension that an impending birth often brought. But today he was the spectator, and it was great. He did one final sweep of the abdomen, checking for placental position, and then removed the wand. "Everything is looking great, Samantha. You can get up now, if you'd like." He reached out a hand to her and she used him like a crane to get back on her feet.

"If one babies in the breech position still, will I have to deliver that way?" she asked as she sat back down.

"Probably not. Under ideal circumstances, and what usually happens, is that once Baby One delivers, then Baby Two will turn as it has twice the amount of room and will deliver head down also. A baby's instincts are nothing short of impressive."

Samantha's face lip up. "That's wonderful to hear. Thank you."

The two women got to their feet to leave, and a strange panic crossed Noah's chest. He couldn't let Tabitha go without attempting another meeting. He hadn't felt anything like this in years.

"Samantha, if you want to confirm your next appointment with Cheryl, I'd just like have a minute to speak to your sister if that's all right?"

"Yes, of course, Doctor," Samantha said, waddling off with the biggest smile on her face.

It was his turn to want to roll his eyes. If Samantha was playing cupid for her sister, then she was doing a good job of it.

"Yes, Doctor?" Tabitha asked, her eyes bright and her attention clear.

"Ah, can we drop the doctor-nurse thing for a minute, Tabitha? It's Noah, please." Her eyelashes fluttered and somewhere in his chest his heart lurched.

"Of course, Noah. What's up?" Her voice had gone strangely high-pitched, and he wondered if that meant she was as self-conscious and nervous as he had become.

"I was wondering if you'd like to meet me for a drink, or perhaps a dinner out sometime?"

Soon, preferably. Please.

"Um... ah..." was all she managed, but she hadn't said 'no' straight off the bat, and he hadn't seen a wedding ring, so he plowed forward.

"I know with our schedules we'll have to book months in advance for even a coffee, but I'm hoping you don't mind dating doctors as well as working with them?" His attempt at light humor was rewarded with eye avoidance and a light laugh.

"Doctor, I mean Noah.... I—"

Warning, warning! Damn.

"Look, I can see this isn't going as well as I'd have hoped, so, I'll give you more information. I know us type-A personalities prefer that. I come from a large family. I have four sisters and two brothers, and most of them are professionals. I work sixty to eighty hours a week, and I've never been married." He waited, hoping that she'd open back up and reveal the radiant personality he'd seen only ten minutes before.

She lifted her gaze and for the first time he saw true vulnerability in her bright blue eyes. "I like being busy. My family's just my mom, dad, sister, and me, but we're very close as you can see." She paused and her hesitation was clear.

"You're married?" he asked, realizing that was probably the first question he should have asked her.

Damn. When did I get so clumsy with dating?

"I was," she admitted. "I went through a pretty rough divorce at the start of the year, and I haven't gotten back out there yet."

The "yet" was what gave him enough hope to move forward with his next query. "Well, I finish work at five, and assuming none of my patients go into labor tonight, how would a seven o'clock dinner suit you? We can do casual and pizza, or fancy with whatever you want."

She bit her lip and didn't say anything as if mulling her options over.

Tentative—a new side to her, and he wasn't sure what to do.

Cheryl appeared out of the corner of his eye and he knew he was out of time.

He pulled his business card out of his back pocket and handed it over. "Well, I've got to eat, so I'll be heading out for dinner tonight, regardless. This has my cell number on it, so if your sister talks you into giving me a chance, give me a call and we'll figure out where to meet."

She took the card with hesitant fingers but held it tight. "Okay. Thank you, Noah." Tabitha turned on her heel and hurried away just as Cheryl ushered in his next patient.

A long sigh left him, and he forced a smile for the pregnant mother entering his office. It had been his first time back at the plate in years, and he wasn't sure if he'd already struck out or not; but he was crossing *everything* that he hadn't.

CHAPTER 5

TABITHA

"You must call him, Tabitha, you simply have to! He's one of the nicest guys I've ever met," her sister argued.

Not to mention one of the hottest, most intelligent, sexiest...

"Yeah, yeah, I know. But I'm not ready to date anyone yet." Tabitha grimaced. Even to her own ears that sounded like a childish cop out.

"Oh, bull crap, Tabby!" Samantha swiped her hand in the air to dismiss Tabitha's sorry excuse. "How long has it been since you've had a man in your bed? A year? I think that's more than enough time, Tabitha. No one's going to accuse you of getting out there too soon!"

Tabitha turned away to turn on gas for the kettle so her sister couldn't see the look on her face. It had been longer than twelve months, unfortunately. Her sex life had died off shortly after their honeymoon, and Tabitha hadn't really been surprised when she'd found out he'd been screwing the ophthalmologist. He had to get it from somewhere, because he hadn't been getting it at home.

"Maybe..." she said, almost to herself as she fiddled with organizing her mug.

"No maybes! I've asked his receptionist about Doctor O'Grady *so* many times and she said he doesn't date! If you've got his attention, then you need to jump on it while you can. And it's Christmas, so you never know. Holiday magic and all that!"

That deserved an eye roll. "Yeah, right. It's such a magical time of the year."

Samantha's hand softly grabbed Tabitha's arm and she turned her toward her sister's concerned face. "I don't want to move knowing you're still sad and alone, Sis. I love you so much and I just want you to be happy. Please, please, *please* take this chance! For me?"

That wasn't a fair move to play.

"It's not like we'll be married and living happily ever after within the next month, Sam."

Her sister rolled her lip down into her famous puppy dog begging face, the one she'd used on Tabitha since they were little.

Tabitha mentally threw up her hands in defeat. She couldn't say no to that. "Fine, I'll call him. But it's just one dinner."

And if he's as nice as he seems, maybe a coffee afterwards as well.

She didn't even allow her brain to indulge in all the pros and cons of dating a physician with an already jam-packed schedule like her own. They hadn't even gotten past the first date yet, so there no point in dragging down her enthusiasm in advance.

She picked up her phone and dialed the number on Noah's business card, her stomach jumping inside her abdomen like a jack rabbit. His voicemail soon picked up and she took quick, short breaths while she answered. "Hi, Noah, it's Tabitha. I just wanted to let you know that I am free for dinner tonight. There's a pizza place about a block from the hospital—Mario's—if you wanted to meet me there at seven? That'd be great. Thank you."

She hung up before her voice rose to a squeal, then she let out a ridiculous gasp that sounded suspiciously like it came from the mouth of a lovesick teenager. "Oh, crap. That was harder than I thought it would be."

Her sister actually clapped. "You did great, Sis. Now, we've got to find something for you to wear. Come, raid my closet. I've been meaning to ask you to take anything that fits you. God knows, I'll never be a size six again!"

Tabitha laughed along with her sister but refused to comment. The last thing she wanted Samantha to do was put extra pressure on herself to get thin after the baby was born.

They made their way into Samantha's walk-in, and she spent the rest of the day going through her fashionable clothes and parading them like a clotheshorse for her little sister. By the time seven o'clock rolled around, Tabitha had already consumed half a bottle of white wine and was decked out in her sister's favorite black dress and heels to keep her confidence as high as possible.

She teetered on the stilettos and alcohol-soaked knees, waiting outside the restaurant for the doctor.

"Whoa, you look amazing," Noah whistled as he walked up to where she stood on the sidewalk outside the restaurant.

"Thank you. I raided my sister's wardrobe and got an Uber to drop me here," she admitted, with what little filter she possessed when totally obliterated by the wine. It'd been way too long since she last had a drink, and it'd hit her hard.

He gave her a lop-sided smile and indicated the restaurant door. "Shall we go in? I'm starving."

They made their way inside and were shown to a quiet booth in the back. The doctor certainly scrubbed up well outside of his work attire. He wore a soft leather jacket, white shirt, and dark blue jeans.

Casual and perfect.

"What sort of pizza do you like?" he asked.

She gazed over the menu, her stomach growling in its need for calories. As usual, she hadn't eaten much that day. Since her divorce, her appetite had evaporated and so had her weight, which was the only reason she fit into her sister's tiny dress. "I eat practically anything except mushrooms and olives."

"Great. So, do you want share a plate? Maybe a seafood gourmet and the *quattro formaggio?*"

She grinned and dropped the menu in relief. "Perfect, thanks. And some garlic bread, if possible?" Her head was spinning a little too much and her decision to loosen up with some wine was fast becoming a less-than-smart idea. "I'm sorry, I'm a little tipsy already. My sister plied me with wine, but the pizza will soon soak it all up."

Noah gave her a proper smile this time. "Dutch courage, huh?"

She nodded. "Yeah, you could say that."

"Well, I'm glad you called. I wasn't sure you would."

She laughed this time. "Yeah, me neither. I haven't exactly been myself this year."

"I can understand that. Divorce can be shockingly painful, especially if you aren't the one wanting the change."

She clenched her hands together in her lap. "Oh, I wanted it, all right. I was the one who filed for divorce. But he was the one cheating, so I suppose he was the one who really wanted out."

"Oh, ouch," he said, his face twisting up in obvious sympathy.

"Yeah. You're telling me," She said, suddenly craving the wine she'd left back at her sister's house. Maybe she ought to order some more after all?

The waiter came up to take their order and Noah ordered their pizzas and then turned to her., "Did you want more wine?" he asked.

She almost said 'yes', but then shook her head at the last moment. She needed to keep her wits about her around this guy. She could already feel herself wanting to pour out her heart to him —something she simply didn't do.

Time to focus on him.

"Tell me more about you, Doctor-Big-Family," she teased.

He laughed out loud at that, and it was such a rich, husky sound that it soothed her soul in a strange, almost blissful way. This was the sort of man she'd always needed in her life.

Happy. Smart. Kind.

"Um... there's not much to tell really. Went to Cal U. I'm thirty-nine."

"Forty next year, huh? Have you got a big party planned?" Forty seemed so far off for her, but in the scheme of things, it probably wasn't. The last year dragging likely made it feel that way.

"God, I hope not. But I have four sisters, so you never know what they'll have in store for me."

She loved the idea that he let the strong women in his family surprise and spoil him. "Okay... then, why aren't you married? Surely your family would have been throwing women at you for decades now?"

"Ha! Well, firstly, yes, you're right. My sisters have a weekly family email blast, and it often includes date recommendations for me."

She sat up straight and looked him in the eye. "You're joking, right?"

They couldn't possibly. How rude would that be?

He burst out laughing and shook his head. "I only wish I were! They're all moms, so I get a list of single mothers from school, neighbors, tennis partners. Basically, if someone is available, they're the first to let me know."

"That is *so* intense! But I suppose they're only trying to help, and even without the whole doctor thing, you're an easy sell to all the moms especially, because you obviously love kids."

He smiled gently. "Yeah, I do."

Something just wasn't adding up with this guy. No one this perfect was single. Was he just a total workaholic? Did he have skeletons in his closet?

Seven illegitimate children tucked away, somewhere?

"So..." she led with, hoping he'd spill the beans earlier, rather than later. She had no defense against a truly good guy, especially when tipsy.

"So...?" he countered.

Do I have to spell it out?

Their food arrived and she grabbed at the crispy garlic bread and eating a piece quickly before continuing with their conversation. She was a real lightweight with alcohol at this weight and needed to be careful she didn't say anything too offensive or unflattering. The last thing she wanted to do was put her foot in it and make things awkward for her sister if things didn't work out.

"So... how are you not married? I seriously can't believe there's an unattached physician who loves kids, has a great family support network, a sense of humor, and your face."

"My face?"

She laughed, disarmed in a heartbeat.

Oops! Hadn't meant to say that.

"Yeah."

He quirked one eyebrow up at her in query.

Heat rose in her cheeks, sending her skin into meltdown. And there was nowhere to hide, so she picked up a glass of water off the table as delicately as she could and buried her face in it, chugging down the icy liquid.

"Well... I don't really know how to answer that, to be honest, Tabitha. College consumed years of my life, as did med school. Then there was a specialist internship, my residency, a private practice, followed by the hospital. I've been so focused on getting where I've wanted to be professionally that now I'm here, well... My social life is unsurprisingly... *very* lacking."

Images of all the doctors she'd worked with over the years flashed before her eyes. "But aren't those bigger hospitals like... incestuous cesspools? Doesn't everyone sleep with everyone else?" She didn't know a single nurse who hadn't slept with at least one specialist.

He laughed with amusement, a sexy smirk on his lips. "Speaking from experience, Tabitha?"

Horrified, she flushed with another hot blush. "No! Not me. I never... fooled around with the doctors. I just know that *a lot* of the others did." And with Noah being handsome, and above all else, a great guy, he would have been practically beating them all off with a stick.

He shrugged and picked up his pizza slice. "I can't say I've been a saint, I just never found anyone I wanted to share my whole life with. I've had girlfriends... but none of them understood my work. They didn't like me being on call twenty-four hours a day or having to work through the holidays."

Her face was cooling so she put down her drink and began to eat, the explosion of creamy garlic across her taste buds a surprising complement to the fresh seafood pizza. "So, you never even got close to being married, then?"

"I did... once," he admitted.

"What happened?" she asked, some insane need to find out

about his romantic past and what that could mean for her, drove her forward. As a woman, she knew she was being foolish by asking such questions. They'd only lead to jealousy and all sorts of crap later, but even so... she had to know.

CHAPTER 6

TABITHA

"She left me for an oncologist who works nine-to-five and flies her around the world every other month," he revealed.

For the first time since she'd met him, Tabitha saw the light go out of Noah's eyes and she didn't like it one single bit. She reached across the table and grabbed his hand, willing him to believe her. "Then she's a fuckwit and didn't deserve you."

That made him explode with laughter, but he didn't pull his hand away.

"I agree."

"I know all specialties have their place in the grand scheme of things, but I'd personally prefer to spend my time birthing babies every day," she said, finally seeing the warmth return to Noah's face. "You're literally helping to bring life into the world, and I think it's beautiful."

"Well, obviously I agree," Noah said with a smile. "Okay... it's *my* turn for the probing questions," he announced.

She slowly withdrew her hand. Now that the tables were turned, she wasn't sure she liked the sound of that, but she couldn't protest after the grilling she'd just given him. "Okay, shoot," she said.

"When was the last time you kissed someone?"

"Oh... um..." That one took her by surprise. "I don't know... a year, maybe?"

Noah slid around the booth, moving closer to her.

Her heart began to hammer in her chest, and she swallowed hard as her throat tightened.

"Well, I think we need to remedy that right now." Noah reached up and cupped her face with the softest of all caresses.

She couldn't help but lean into it. It felt *so* right. "Whatever you say, Doctor," she whispered.

He moved closer still and his nose brushed by hers.

She followed her instincts and tilted up her chin to meet his lips as they pressed against hers.

He held her there, neither rushing her, nor pressing deep He kept her there, in the moment, just tasting her—savoring her like she was a fine wine or the sweetest of treats.

It lasted longer than she thought it would. Her eyes drifted closed and her hands moved up to his shoulders to hold him there. Then a helpless moan escaped from her throat unbidden.

He pulled her closer, separating her lips so that he could sweep his tongue inside her mouth and taste her properly.

She groaned against his lips as his flavor swept her mouth. He tasted of Heaven and sin all at once. He was simply pure, hot male in the truest sense. She let her tongue meet his in a dance as old as time and reveled in it, losing herself to the kiss.

Then, before she was ready, he began to draw away, kissing her lips gently closed before pulling away.

She blinked her eyes open slowly, the dream-like quality of the kiss something she would always remember.

He cleared his throat and gazed at her with fire burning in the embers of his eyes. "That was far more than I intended. I apologize."

He's apologizing? For what?

"Don't apologize, please."

He looked at her sidelong. "You aren't mad at me?"

She huffed on a startled laugh, bringing her fingers to her lips in memory. "Hardly. That was beautiful."

Noah growled low in his throat a moment before he swooped on her to claim another kiss.

This time she was ready for him. She pressed his lips open and slanted her mouth to better taste him. The fire in her flesh lit up her whole body and made her yearn for his hands on her skin as her own hands strayed up and down his muscular arms.

It's been so long...

A stifled groan emanated from him as he pulled away unexpectedly, though the look on his comically frustrated face made it clear he *really* didn't want to. "Please don't do that," he begged sheepishly. "I won't be able to stand up for another five minutes now." His eyes dropped to his crotch momentarily and he cleared his throat, then reached for his water.

A grin tugged up her lips on both sides and a wonderfully happy mood saturated her entire being. "That good, huh?" she joked.

He growled back, his lower lip slack with lust.

He growled back! Wow.

She'd never caused such a reaction in a man before. It was strangely intoxicating to have that kind of power. After her douchebag ex, she never would have believed she was capable of eliciting a response like that. Especially not from a gorgeous, educated, handsome doctor.

"You have *no* idea how much I want to take you back to my house and kiss every inch of this delectable little body of yours."

She grabbed her glass of water and chugged it down, offering a nervous laugh afterward. It was the only thing she could think of to stop herself from asking him to do exactly that!

Noah cleared his throat. "Ah, did that make you uncomfortable? I'm sorry."

She reached out for his arm and squeezed his flesh. He must think she was made of glass the way he apologized all the time. And maybe she appeared that way sometimes, but she wasn't. "Don't ever be sorry for wanting to kiss me or anything else. My ex-husband stopped wanting me within the first few weeks of our marriage. Maybe he never really wanted me in the first place, I don't know. But it's nice to feel wanted." Her courage deserted her as the words flowed. She'd barely exposed any of her pain to anyone except her sister and her mother.

"Well, I want you—more than I should," Noah said, his eyes gleamed with honesty and truth. "I'm not like this with just anyone, Tabitha."

Tabitha grabbed at her courage with both hands, swallowing hard at the tightness in her chest. After being alone for so long, it was hard to trust, hard to believe. But there was something special about this man, and ignoring every instinct that told her to plow forward would be beyond stupid.

Instinct exists for a reason.

"I know what you mean," she said quietly as she licked her

lips. "I didn't think I was ready for anything like this, after everything I've been through... but your kisses have me aching in places I'd forgotten even existed."

That same fire she felt blazing in her belly flashed in Noah's eyes and she leaned forward with all the bravery she had, eager to know which move he'd play next.

CHAPTER 7

NOAH

Noah had no idea how he was going to contain himself for the rest of the night. This beautiful, angelic, broken creature brought out his most protective instincts. As well as his most base desires. He wanted nothing more than to tuck her into his arms and carry her home, lay her in his bed and make her cry out with pleasure until she forgot she'd ever been mistreated.

She looked beyond magnificent in that little black dress and her towering heels. And he found himself yearning to taste the skin at her throat and trail his hands over her slender figure. He could only imagine what mouth-watering beauty remained hidden behind that scrap of silky black fabric. The thought teased him and had him fidgeting his feet under the table as he worked had to keep his desire under wraps.

She needs to be wanted, that much is obvious.

Whoever the asshole was that she'd been married to... it was evident he deserved to choke on his own damn tongue. Instead of making his wife feel loved and desired, he'd betrayed her in the worst possible way. He couldn't even fathom how a man could stray so quickly after marriage. Was he mad? A sex-pest? Did he ever truly love her? While they were questions he'd likely never have answers to, he couldn't help but wonder.

Who would trade in this beautiful soul for another?

He reached across the table and took her hand in his. That small, physical connection would have to be enough for now. Making love to her, he already knew, would be like skating on thin ice for him. If he didn't want to lose his heart in the process, he was going to have hold back. And that was going to be extremely difficult with a woman like this; pure, smart, caring, and loving.

She demanded more, and his old, tired heart was ready to give its all.

He cleared his throat. "You know, I haven't dated anyone in more months than I can count, but when you went to leave my office today, I couldn't fathom the idea of never seeing you again. It made me panic, to be honest, and that's not a feeling I'm well acquainted with. Everything I do in life requires a calm, logical, and cool demeanor. But you awoke something in me I can't deny."

Tabitha smiled at him with a radiance that made his admission all the more worthwhile. "I'm glad you asked me out to dinner," she answered. "I would never have had the guts to ask you, myself."

That hinted at a mutual attraction. "But you wanted to?" he pressed, his curiosity getting the better of him.

"Of course! I had to go sit down on that chair today during the ultrasound because standing next to you was a bit more than difficult. It wasn't just because of the twins' sex."

That made him chuckle. He'd thought he'd been the only one affected by the attraction burning between them. "Oh, really? Weak kneed, were you?" he teased playfully.

She smiled softly and dropped her gaze. "It was more like... an aching..."

His gut tightened with lust once again and he stifled another groan. "I can't take you home tonight, can I? Damn."

Her gaze flew up to meet his and she bit her lip, as though scared to admit to what she wanted to divulge.

He could only imagine how she must feel having been abstinent for so long. So, he pushed forward. "I know you aren't supposed to want that on the first date, but God, you're beautiful, Tabitha. I'm going to have to go home and have a long, cold shower after this."

She giggled in a way that reminded him of a lovesick teen and she squeezed his hand. Her delight and attraction were honest and sweet.

Damn, I want to sweep her off her feet.

And although the prospect of very blue balls was in his future, he was glad for the compliment it paid her.

"Me too, I think," she said, chewing on her lip and blushing.

His stomach gurgled and he looked down at the cooling pizza. "Well, for now, let's finish this food off, and then we can talk about something totally non-sexual so things can, ah, settle down. Let's find a neutral subject. Like, maybe tell me something funny about your work?"

That should keep my mind out of the bedroom.

Tabitha launched into an animated discussion about their hospital's podiatrist, not naming names, of course, detailing all his weird foibles and quirks that had her and the other nurses in stitches.

It's always the podiatrist!

She had him laughing and smiling all night long and for a while, he managed to forget that his life was dedicated to the service of others. Being with her consumed him in a way he'd never felt before. It was refreshing and heady and absolutely unexpected. So, when it was finally time to kiss her goodnight, he held her too long and allowed himself to linger, tasting her too much.

For a man who'd believed his only course in life was a successful career, and that the prospect of true romance was not on the cards for him— today may well have proven him entirely wrong! And if he had anything to do with it, he'd be seeing Samantha's sister a lot more in future. Because you didn't stumble upon a woman like Tabitha every day. She was special and no matter how difficult dating proved to be with a nurse who worked just as many hours as he did, he'd move mountains for the chance.

When Noah got home and stepped into his cold shower, he shivered as the water hit his hot skin and beaded down his body to swirl down the drain. No matter how hard he tried, there was no way he was getting any sleep tonight unless he got comfortable and took matters into his own hands.

CHAPTER 8

TABITHA

"So... when are you seeing him again?" Sam asked Tabitha as they walked around the local department store, choosing placemats and Christmas tree decorations for their family luncheon.

"Tomorrow night, actually. We're squeezing in a dinner between his day shift and my night shift."

And although it had been five days since they'd last seen each other, he hadn't been absent. In fact, Noah had called her every single day, just to check how her day had been and to share funny tales of his obstetric adventures.

Far too quickly he was becoming a daily happiness that she

was going to find very hard to give up if she ever had to. He was the breath of fresh air she needed in her life, and she feared that if she lost him, it'd feel like suffocation even if she was standing out under a clear, cloudless sky.

"You two are going to be like ships in the night if you ever move in together," Samantha remarked.

Tabitha shrugged as her sister chose a heap of decorations for her to load into the shopping cart, and she didn't even care. Bring on tinsel disaster! She was in too good a mood to worry about holly. "I think you're getting a little ahead of yourself, Sam. We've only been on one date so far."

Sam rolled her eyes. "Oh, come on. How about all the phone calls? At his age, Dr. O'Grady is not fooling around. He knows what he wants and so do you. I say marriage is on the cards in the next six months, a baby a year after that, and then you'll be back on track."

This time it was Tabitha who rolled her eyes. Women and their ridiculous timelines! She'd once adhered to such a societally accepted schedule and all it had done was see her married to the wrong guy and forced her to bust her ass to keep what remained of her life afloat.

I'm never going to be that girl again.

"I don't think it'll work out like that, Sam, but surprisingly enough... I'm enjoying spending time with him."

"Who's surprised?" Sam asked with all the authority of an older sister—as if we'd suddenly traded roles. "He's hot, intelligent, single, and has an income that could support you and your household without your needing to work the ridiculous number of hours you do," she reasoned as she continued to browse.

Next topic.

"I like my work, and so does he."

But a few less shifts would probably be nice. It can get damn stressful and overwhelming.

Sam scoffed. "Yeah, right. Tell me you wouldn't love to be Mrs. Noah O'Grady and sit at home tending babies and the house."

Tabitha growled at her sister in frustration. "No, I would not, Sam! Stop assuming that I want everything you do. Yeah, I'd like my very own happily ever after, but mine doesn't look the same as yours."

For starters, she was never planning on giving up her nursing career. She'd worked too hard for too long to be good at her job. Besides, lots of moms worked part-time to cultivate a work-life balance that suited them. Also, keeping her career meant she'd never be screwed over-not completely anyway. She'd always have a means of supporting herself and paying the bills. And that kind of knowledge and personal security was worth more than a Cinderella style dream.

"Excuse me," a woman interrupted as she walked closer. "Did you say Noah O'Grady?"

Oh God, it's one of his sisters. Just look at those eyes! Shit.

"Ah, yes... he's my sister's obstetrician," Tabitha offered, knowing that wasn't the line she should have gone with, but she felt helpless to clarify.

"And my sister's dating him!" Sam threw back with a shameless grin.

Tabitha tried to smile but struggled beneath the weight of his sister's stare. She mustered up the courage and pushed forward. It's not like the situation could get any more unexpected or strange. "You must be one of his four sisters," she said. "It's nice to meet you. I'm Tabitha."

The woman, who looked about her age, but wiser in the ways of the world, looked her up and down with a keen eye. "How on Earth did you recognize me?" she asked.

Tabitha shrugged. "It's your eyes, mostly." And the way she spoke, the way she parted her hair, and the fact that Noah had said he had four sisters all of whom lived locally. She supposed it was only a matter of time before they ran into one another.

The woman nodded slowly, as though assessing the situation. "I'm Millie and it's nice to meet you, too. Noah doesn't bring many of his girlfriend's home to meet us."

Her tone made Tabitha want to grind her teeth and she had to resist the urge to walk away. After being defensive of her choices for so long, she didn't like the feeling of being judged or interrogated by someone who didn't even know her. "I'm not his girlfriend. We've only been on one date, so please excuse my sister's overly enthusiastic attitude. But he's a lovely man and I'm really enjoying getting to know him."

"Really?" Millie asked, her eyebrows rising high on her forehead. "Other than the fact he's gorgeous and a doctor who makes a fortune, what makes him so special?"

Tabitha knew she was being baited, but she couldn't stop herself rising to the hook like a fish in a pond. She wasn't going to allow anyone to assume she was a gold-digger. She was a woman with her own career and liked Noah for genuine reasons. "Well, there's his infectious smile and his amazing laugh. His tenderness and his gentle touch. The way he cares for his patients and his staff. I've seen firsthand just how much his staff adores him, and that adoration would not have been won easily. I work in the same field and know what that crowed can be like."

Millie softened in the way butter melts on a griddle. She grabbed Tabitha's hands and squeezed them between her own with a smile. "I really hope we get to meet you at a family event in the future," she said, her voice warm, and then she walked away.

Tabitha stared after her with the strangest feeling. It was like doom and awe mixed together in a perfect storm. If they were all as intense as that, it was no wonder Noah was still single at thirty-nine years old. His sisters were proverbial gatekeepers!

Sam grabbed her attention by tapping Tabitha on the arm. "Whoa. Um, clue me in. But what was that all about?"

She shrugged, still watching as Millie meandered away. "Noah comes from a really big family, and they're pretty protective of one another from what I've heard."

"Well, obviously," Samantha smirked and shook her head at the impromptu meet and greet.

Tabitha shook herself, adrenaline still zinging through her bloodstream. She felt like a kid with a sugar rush, on the rush was one of annoyance that grew into palpable anger. The unspoken accusations Noah's sister had made whirled around her head, and the more she thought about them, the more incensed she got.

Who did Millie think she was? And how dare she assume that Tabitha was some sort of gold-digger after his money? She barely knew Noah! Not to mention Tabitha had more self-respect than that. She wanted a man, but she didn't need a man. And that was a damn crucial distinction. Obviously, Millie had warmed up toward her in the end, having her heard her reasons, but still.

What happened to giving people the benefit of the doubt?

"Let's go down this aisle," Samantha called as she waddled through the festive and cheery lights section.

Tabitha wasn't as easily distracted, unfortunately, and she couldn't shake the feeling of inevitability that invaded her senses. She was on a course with this man, for better or worse. Through a sheer stroke of luck she'd found someone worth not only dating, but worth loving, and probably worth marrying. And all after she'd sworn off men forever.

Hours later Tabitha was getting ready for work when her phone rang. It was Noah. She picked the call up with a smile in her voice. "Hey, you."

"Hey, yourself. I am so sorry for Millie. I know what a bitch she can be if she gets a bee in her bonnet."

Tabitha smiled to herself. "After almost a decade of nursing in the ER department, I can handle an over-protective woman or two. Don't worry." She'd handled a lot worse before, it had just been a while since she'd dealt with a more personal confrontation.

Noah groaned. "Oh God, I hope you don't meet the other three out and about while shopping for Christmas stuff. They're even worse."

His voice was so reminiscent of how Samantha spoke about her, that it convinced Tabitha right there and then, in that moment, how devoted Noah truly was to his family. "I'm sure I'll survive it," she assured him. "Besides, it's nice to see how close you guys are."

Her ex-husband had been estranged from his only sister, and that had always sat uncomfortably with Tabitha. Sure, he'd blamed it all on his sister at the time, of course, but looking back now, it was obvious who was really to blame.

Once a liar, always a liar.

"Yeah, but they're the main reason that my ex-girlfriend left me. She said it was because of them. And I don't want them driving you away, too."

They wouldn't be able to do that, because Tabitha already knew the truth. That his ex-girlfriend was a selfish little bitch who didn't care about him at all. Family protected you because they loved you, they didn't drive people away who cared about you. It was more than likely that they suspected exactly what type of person she was and made sure she couldn't get her claws into Noah properly.

"Oh, you haven't met the rest of my family yet," she said with a laugh in her voice. "We're smaller, but I bet my sister and mother could give your sisters a run for their money! They're like a storm in a teacup when they're together. It's full on."

There was a strange, pregnant pause before Noah spoke next. "So, you're not mad?" he asked hesitantly.

Tabitha's brow furrowed. "Of course not. Why would I be?" In retrospect, she kind of loved how fierce his sister was. It reminded her of Sam. And it also proved to be a great compliment to Noah's character, because nasty people didn't inspire such love and protection from others.

"Well... I..." he didn't seem to have a good reason to worry it seemed, beyond panic.

She saved him from having to pick up the threads. "I'm really looking forward to seeing you tomorrow. Where are we going?"

"Oh, it's a surprise," he said, his voice brighter. "I'll pick you up about four, if that still works?"

"Yeah, should be fine."

"Great, I'll see you then, Tabby."

"Bye, Noah."

Tabitha hung up the phone as butterflies fluttered their wings madly inside her belly. The excitement filled her up until she was forced to stifle a squeal that slipped from her lips.

Noah likes me, he really does.

And with her heart racing and the butterflies causing chaos within her, amazingly, she knew she *really* liked him too...

CHAPTER 9

NOAH

Four o'clock rolled around and Noah pulled up in front of Tabitha's house. It was a nice home, but huge for only one person. And although he hadn't seen inside it yet, he knew it was built as a family home. It was nothing like his chic, inner city apartment.

Which, in his mind, meant that Tabitha had originally planned on having a family—a big one—when she'd first married the asshole. Thankfully she hadn't gone through with having children with her ex, or she likely would have gotten stuck with him for decades, like so many other women before her.

He knocked on the front door and within a moment the door was opening for him.

"Hi," Tabitha said, greeting him with her beautiful, cheerful smile.

He couldn't help the way he reacted next. He instinctively stepped up and took her into his arms, her body a little stiff against him as he embraced her. "Hi, back," he said before he pressed a kiss to her lips.

To his surprise she quickly pulled away.

"Ah, what's wrong?" he asked, confused by her response. He'd thought they were onto a good thing here, and that included socially acceptable displays of affection in public.

"Oh nothing!" she tried to assure him. "I just don't want the neighbors to see." Without further explanation she hurried off the porch and across to his car.

He walked slowly behind her, annoyance building in his gut. Why wouldn't she want the neighbors to see that she was dating someone new? Maybe because they thought she was married still? But why would she care about that? She might be fragile in her own way, but that seemed an odd thing to worry about.

"So, where are we off to?" she asked, getting into the passenger side.

Like the gentleman he'd been raised to be, he closed the door for her and strode around the car. "You'll see," he said simply. He got in and turned on the ignition, but curiosity was eating him up inside. He had to ask. "What's with the embarrassment on the porch? Do you have a private detective who lives next door or something?"

She looked away and out the window. "No, it's not that. It's just that..." she trailed off and didn't seem to want to continue.

"Just what?" he prompted. He wanted to know what the problem was. He didn't exactly have a timeline for this relationship. Hell, he hadn't planned it at all. But he didn't want to be with someone who was embarrassed to even be seen with him or had some deep dark secrets they'd failed to reveal.

Tabitha sighed heavily. "It's the old lady next door. She's still harping on about how divorce is a sin. She says all men cheat and that it's normal and so on. She thinks I'm the terrible one for kicking my husband out."

Noah sighed internally with relief.

Is that all? Stupid old biddy and her archaic beliefs. How dare she push her old-fashioned values on someone like Tabitha?

He reached over and rested his hand on her thigh. The muscles tightened and tensed beneath his hand, but he left it there, determined to make his point. "She sounds like a bitch, Tabby, and you don't deserve that in your life."

She heaved a sigh and turned back to look at him, a small sparkle had returned to her eyes. "Yeah, I agree," she said. "Those views are outdated, and I do deserve better."

They drove on in companionable silence, through the streets of Seattle until they pulled up outside his mother's huge house.

"Wow. Where are we?" she asked, leaning forward to look up at the house through the windshield. "It's incredible," she breathed.

"This is my parent's place. My nephew is having his fourth birthday party today and I promised I'd drop in if I could get away from work." He watched her face carefully.

She just stared through the glass, a strangely pensive look on her face.

"Bad idea?" he asked.

"No, it's a lovely idea, but, uh... I would have probably worn something different if I'd known I was attending a little boy' birthday party." She gestured down to her pencil skirt and silk blouse with a grimace.

He grinned in response. "You look incredibly beautiful and

sexy, and I can't wait to introduce you to my crazy family. You said you could handle them, yeah?"

This would be a baptism by fire for the both of them. He didn't want to go down the same road he had with Kerrie. They'd endured years of fighting, and over what? The mere fact that she never wanted to see his family—and they couldn't stand her. He couldn't do that again. Besides, he trusted his mother's instincts regarding women, so if she approved of Tabitha today, then he could relax a little. He'd know for sure he was dating a truly good woman.

Tabitha grinned at him and undid her seat belt. "So, is this your idea of fun, then? Tossing me in the deep end, huh?"

He smiled back.

Smart and damn sexy.

"Baptism by fire," he offered with a wink.

"Let's go, then."

They hopped out of the car, and he took her hand as they crossed the street.

"So... I'm your... what, exactly?" she asked as he led her up the front steps.

"We can just say friend for now, if you like?"

She nodded rapidly, her gaze filled with relief.

And he knew he'd read her correctly. She wasn't ready for titles, but she seemed genuinely ready and excited to meet his crazy crew and what more could he want for then that? He lifted his hand to knock on the door.

Without warning she grabbed his arm to stop him.

"What if they don't like me?" she asked, a note of panic in her voice.

He found her earnest reaction endearing. The fact she cared what kind of first impression she'd make with his family only cemented his growing feelings for her. He laughed at her and knocked *hard*. "I have no doubt they'll love you. Just be yourself."

He didn't really know what had possessed him to bring home a date after such a short acquaintance, but it felt right. And after too many years of following his gut above all else, he trusted it now more than ever.

The door swung open, and his mother appeared. "Noah! I'm so glad you made it." She grabbed him up in a hug, then drew away, her gaze dancing over to focus on Tabitha. "And this is?" she asked.

"Mom, this is Tabitha. Tabitha, may I present the matriarch of our family."

"It's really nice to meet you. I'm so sorry I didn't bring a gift. Noah didn't tell me we were coming to a birthday party." Tabitha rattled off, her sweet nervousness clear as day.

His mother smiled with genuine happiness. "Oh, don't worry about that," she said, waving her hand in a dismissive gesture. "That little boy has got more presents than a kid knows what to do with! Come on in and have something to eat. Though, I hope you're not a vegetarian?" his mother queried with a mock scowl.

Noah rolled his eyes. His last girlfriend had been a vegetarian, and a very outspoken one, at that. It'd honestly bordered on belligerent and abusive at times.

"Oh, no, not at all. You can't do double shifts at the hospital on salad," Tabitha joked.

His mother's face lit up again. "Oh, you work with Noah?"

"I work at St. John of God in the ER department," Tabitha clarified.

"As a nurse?" his mother pushed.

"Yes," Tabitha answered.

His mother took her by the arm and led her over the threshold and into the family room. "I was a nurse myself. I did thirty-six years at St. Mary's."

And off they went, just like that, they were thick as thieves.

Tabitha handled his family beautifully for the whole evening, laughing and talking with them as if she'd known them for years.

His mother sent glowing praise her way whenever it was warranted and even his sisters seemed to like her once they'd given her a chance to speak for herself.

Noah stood with his brothers for most of the afternoon but kept an eye out for any signs of trouble.

By the time the sun had gone down and they'd both stuffed themselves full of dinner, drinks, and then birthday cake, it was finally time to go home.

"Thank you *so* much for having me," Tabitha gushed at his parents graciously.

His parents stepped forward to hug his new 'friend'. Even his dad. Which was huge deal for a man who barely shook hands with anyone.

"Feel free to drop in anytime," they told her.

As they bid them goodbye and walked away he couldn't help but laugh. "Well, you certainly wrapped them around your little finger," he told her, chuckling as they got into the car.

"They're really beautiful people." Tabitha sighed, a content smile settling on her lips.

"Yeah, just don't get on the wrong side of an argument with them. They're ruthless once they get started and they're sore losers," he warned her.

She slid her hand onto his thigh like it was the most natural thing in the world and giggled. "I consider myself forewarned."

Noah started the car but couldn't bear the thought of having to take her home. "Are you working this evening?" he asked.

"Not anymore," she answered, flashing him a coy grin. "One of the nurses wanted a swap, so now I'm doing an afternoon double tomorrow." She fell quiet and gazed at him intently. "How about you?"

"Well, I'm always on call of course, but I'm not working until ten tomorrow." More silence followed and as the time ticked by Noah decided to grab the proverbial bull by the horns. "My apartment's only ten minutes or so from here. Would you like to come back for a drink?" he asked.

She chewed on her lips, an adorable habit she had when she was nervous.

He put a hand up to wave off any confusion. "No pressure, of course. I just don't feel like ending this date yet. I really enjoy your company."

She nodded quickly, pursing her lips and not meeting his gaze. "I'd love to see your place."

He didn't need any more of a 'yes' than that. He turned the car onto the main road and headed back to his apartment. He owned a crisp and minimalist two-bedroom penthouse on a small block near the hospital. It was convenient and he thought it was a good investment. He pulled into the underground parking garage and turned the ignition off.

Together, they hopped out of the car and walked toward the elevator.

He swiped his access card, pressed the button, and turned to face her. "I have red wine or white. What's your preference?"

Tabitha didn't answer. Instead, she took control of the situation and kissed him passionately, pressing her warm body against his, and holding his face with her soft hands.

He responded in kind, wrapping his arms around her waist and exploring her mouth with his tongue.

She moaned in her throat in that delightful way she did.

He thrust himself against her pelvis, unable to deny the building hunger within him.

The doors dinged open, and they broke apart temporarily, lucky to find the lift unoccupied.

"Let's go," he growled, tugging her into the elevator after him. He tapped his key card again that would allow them access to his private floor. Noah didn't want the heat between them to diminish at all, so he pressed her up against one of the mirrored walls and kissed her as deeply as he craved. There were so many things he wanted to do to her, all at once. But he contented himself with holding her beautiful face in his hands and tasting her perfect lips.

Her response was exquisite, passionate, and unguarded. She grabbed at his shoulders and held him tightly to her as if he were the air she needed to breathe.

He loved her passion and her honesty. It was clear she wanted him every bit as much as he wanted her. He could see it in the way she moved, in the way her body responded to his, and by the way she looked at him. There were no games with Tabitha, for which he was grateful. Or at least, there hadn't been, so far. Only time would tell if she was playing a longer game or if he'd stumbled upon the real deal of his dreams.

The doors to the elevator finally *dinged* open and he tugged her out and straight into his condo. He locked his front door behind them and brought her into the warmth of his open-plan, expansive living space.

She put a hand on his chest and pushed him down, so that he landed on the couch. Then she pulled her skirt higher up her thighs and straddled him in a truly sexy, dominant way that made his cock throb painfully hard against the zipper of his jeans. Heedless of his discomfort she kissed him slowly, keeping her eyes open so that he was forced to look directly into her soul as she snuck the tip of her tongue into his mouth.

He groaned at her palpable need and grabbed for her delicious body, her smooth rounded hips, and her slender waist, before pulling her blouse out of her skirt and sliding his hands up under her top. Her firm breasts filled his hands, the lacy bra pressing into his fingers and keeping her naked flesh from his touch.

With a knowing look in her eye, she pulled back and unbuttoned her blouse, one agonizingly slow button at a time. The fabric soon fell away, and her body revealed itself to him in all its perfect splendor.

"You are so beautiful, Tabitha," he breathed.

She smiled shyly and ran her hands up his arms, grabbing onto his shirt. "Can I see you, too?"

A grin spread across his face as excitement filled his blood and rushed to his groin with even more purpose. "Absolutely."

CHAPTER 10

TABITHA

Tabitha's heart fluttered in her chest like a caged canary, desperate to break free of its confines. She burned *everywhere*. In her belly and deep between her thighs where she longed for him to be. Her nipples tightened and tingled against her lace bra, alert and desperate for his touch.

This hunger was new—a voracious appetite the likes of which she'd never possessed. But as soon as Noah had kissed her tonight, she'd known then and there that she didn't want to stop until they were both fully sated. If she even knew what that was like anymore. It had been too long since her last man-induced orgasm, and the thought of it had every inch of her yearning with desire.

She tugged at his shirt, encouraging him to lose it and fast.

He pulled it over his head in that sexy way only men seemed capable of.

His chest was finally revealed, and she sighed at the beauty before her. So much muscle and so little hair. He'd been hiding the perfect body from her from the very start!

He is just divine. He has a body to rival Apollo!

She dipped her head and pressed a kiss to his lips as she allowed her hands to wander over his pecs, her fingertips teasing his tiny nipples as they passed in their exploration.

Noah growled low in his throat and grabbed her hips, thrusting against her matching lacy panties.

A deep pang of lust tugged inside her and she couldn't take it anymore. She slid off his lap and held out her hand with more confidence than she'd ever felt. Tabitha wanted to be *so* much closer to him than this, and the discomfort of the couch was not what she craved. "Can we go to your bedroom?" she breathlessly.

"Of course," her gorgeous doctor answered. He took her hand and rose to his feet, tugging her in the opposite direction of the front door.

Then, entirely unwelcomed, fears began to creep into her mind, daring her to second guess herself, to call this off before she was in over her head. Deep down she recognized that she was crazy for doing this. It was too early in the relationship.

We barely know each other...

And even if it wasn't too early, per say, her Ex had always said she was bad at this—the sex part. It had been humiliating to hear as well as degrading. He'd made her feel so small. She'd always wondered how she could be bad at it when it was such a universal act. Surely, it was all instinct. Either way, he'd crushed her soul and confidence and now it was her least favorite aspect of a relationship. Or it had been, up until this point.

What if Noah thinks I'm terrible at this as well?

Her heart raced and her breathing became rapid as the hurts of the past tried to re-burrow their way in. But as Noah smiled at her and drew her into his modern bedroom, she put her foot down and swallowed her fears.

She'd already conquered so many of the insecurities her ex had implanted in her, this year. This would be just another ghost laid to rest. She knew she was a loving person as well as an attentive one. Surely, she couldn't be too terrible. And besides, she was an adult and more than willing to learn with the right man, especially if there was passion, love and patience; rather than ridicule, judgement, and pain.

The ultimate truth of the matter was that she didn't want to be anywhere else except right here with Noah. So, for better or worse, she was throwing herself back into the saddle and life again, wholeheartedly.

I can't let fear dominate me.

Noah pulled back the dark comforter on the bed to reveal crisp sheets, then tugged at his clothes. His jeans dropped onto the floor, as he kicked off his shoes and socks. And... he didn't wear underwear, apparently.

Tabitha swallowed hard and squeezed her thighs together as desire pulsed hungrily within her.

Oh, my God.

Noah's fully erect cock jutted out proudly toward her, like the needle on a compass pointing to the direction in which the ship must go. And it seemed abundantly clear that she was to be the harbor.

Noah smiled at her with a cockiness she hadn't expected. "Your turn, beautiful."

With trembling, unsteady hands, she unzipped her skirt and let it slide to the floor. She'd worn the prettiest underwear she owned—a slinky pair of black lace panties and matching bra— not because she'd known they'd end up here tonight. But if she was honest, she'd certainly hoped for some sort of intimacy with him.

Tabitha was hardly an expert on sex, but she found that a man's style of making love told her everything she'd need to know about him. It sounded strange, but it revealed things about a man's character. Whether he was selfish or giving, or whether he was impatient or willing to go the extra mile. In the past, she'd ignored such instinctual warnings. Now, her wiser self knew how important it was to pay heed to those innate cues and act according to her gut.

She only wished she'd followed those rules in her past. But tonight would be her second chance and reveal to her whether Noah was a man worth loving. And if he was, she was *all* in. This time around she wasn't interested in society's opinions of what was right or wrong. She'd listen to her heart and her gut, because too often the mind could be swayed against its will.

"Come here," Noah said, breaking into her reverie with the beckoning crook of his finger.

She was not going to lie, she found that simple come-hither move undeniably sexy. So, dredging up her inner strength she met his gaze and took her time as she slowly and seductively walked the few feet that separated them.

Noah grabbed her as soon as she was within touching distance, kissing her passionately. He swept her up into his arms and lay her down on the soft, but firm mattress as though she weighed nothing at all.

Breathing hard, her eyes never leaving his, she shuffled back up the bed so that her head was settled into the lush collection of silk-covered pillows.

Noah slid down on top of her, his perfect, hard, and muscular form melding against her as if they were made for one another.

And for the first time in her life, she moaned with deep pleasure as the weight of her lover pressed her down satisfyingly into the mattress. She needed him *so* much, she could scarcely find the words in her mind to express it. Though, given Noah hadn't been alone quite so long as her, he might not understand the true depth of her need.

For too long she'd been alone, feeling unwanted, undesirable, and unloved. It was beyond amazing just how much Noah already filled her cup. He was a good man, and she needed him *now*. Without a moment's hesitation she wrapped her legs around his naked waist and reveled in the feel of his hot skin between her thighs.

He kissed her neck, peppering her skin with the caress of his lips, tasting her flesh as he went, inching lower with every second.

Tabitha gasped, arched her back and raised herself toward him, driven by the feeling of her body's joy.

Noah kissed his way further down her body, navigating a slow trail of discovery to her lace-bound breasts.

She arched her back more deeply to give him access to her bra clasps and he eagerly took the opportunity. The black lace slid away like a breathless whisper and Tabitha valiantly fought the need to cover herself.

Her breasts were so much smaller since she'd lost weight due to the stress of her divorce, but Noah didn't seem to care.

He made enthusiastic purring sounds and little growls as he nuzzled her flesh and suckled at her pert nipples with deep, tongue-swirling pulls.

She gasped anew as arrows of pleasure shot through her, aiming for some inner target at her core. Lost in her pleasure, she let go of her inhibitions and moaned, permitting herself the wild abandon of making noises that, in her past life, would have embarrassed her or earned her a reprimand. She arched her back even higher, thrusting her hot, aching flesh into his mouth in the hopes he'd continue pleasuring, rather than moving on.

And to her great delight, Noah was in no rush, which

surprised her. Instead, he teased and lavished the first breast with ample desire, and then the other, taking his time to elicit even more throaty, strained moans from her. Then, releasing her nipple from his teeth, he looked up at her and smiled.

Her heart broke in half in an instant. She saw such beautiful, and genuine happiness in his eyes. She'd never seen anything like it. It seemed like he was really *seeing*, admiring, and appreciating her. There was no feeling that he was just fucking her because he could or even because he wanted to. It wasn't that simple or brazen. Somehow that look in his eyes spoke volumes. What she saw there said that this meant something.

She lifted a hand and gently stroked the side of his face. If there was such a thing as 'falling in love,' the way they described it in literature and movies... she was fast toppling down that hill, and she could only hope it didn't hurt when she hit the bottom.

Drawing her attention back to the present, he gently lowered himself and kissed her belly. He winked at her in the most deliciously deviant way and kept moving down her body, going up onto his knees and tugging down her flimsy underwear at the same time.

She took a deep breath as she lifted her hips to help him. She'd gotten waxed the other day at her sister's insistence, and for the first time in her life, she was damn happy she had. Even though hair down there was natural and something she readily accepted as a woman and a nurse, being hairless and smooth made her feel clean and comfortable when it came to intimacy.

Noah slid down onto his belly, his face very near to most sensitive parts of her.

Panic rose within her, and she tilted her pelvis away from him. Her ex-husband had *hated* doing that to her. He'd always said that she smelled bad, no matter how clean she made herself, and it had made her feel brutally self-conscious about that part of herself ever since.

God, what if he thinks I smell, too? I'll cry if he says anything!

"You don't have to," she interjected. "Honestly, it's fine." She began to sit up and push back at his shoulders, encouraging him to abandon that idea and instead hopefully pursue sex.

Noah didn't respond with words, he simply grabbed her legs, pushed them apart, and licked her with his wickedly hot, wet tongue.

"Oh, God," she breathed as she lay back against the mattress and covered her face with her hands. Tabitha wasn't used to being paid this sort of attention and there was something so skin-crawlingly embarrassing about him doing this to her. Did he feel like he had to?

But Noah continued to lavish her with his hungry affections, smashing her doubts like shards of broken glass, and her feelings on the matter began to change. His magic tongue skimmed over her flesh relentlessly, around and around where she was most sensitive.

Shots of pleasure whispered through her body, starting deep in her belly, before burning its way along the backs of her legs like a fire from within. Moans erupted from her throat as he flicked his tongue from her clit to her core until she was sure she would die. Heat flowed up her face, and her breathing became labored, forcing her to toss, arch, and writhe against the pillows.

"Please come up to me," she begged. She wasn't ready for this. She'd never felt anything like it, and it almost frightened her. For someone as educated on the body as a nurse, she felt like she was learning about her own for the first time. She desperately grabbed for his head and attempted to drag him up.

But he refused, and instead defiantly wrapped his lips around her clitoris and suckled for several long, agonizing moments.,

She gasped and clamped his head with her thighs as impossible sensations assaulted her.

Jesus Christ! That feels fucking incredible. I had no idea.

She whimpered and whined, unable to stop the sounds that spilled from her lips. This kind of ecstasy was almost like torture. She wanted it to go on forever, and yet a part of her begged for release, for it to be over.

Then, just when she thought she could take no more, he finally came up to her and kissed her neck as he lined their bodies up once again.

Relief of a different kind swept through her and she greedily wrapped her arms and legs around his body, holding him close. Tabitha wanted to be possessed by him, desperately and she was *more* than ready. If Noah didn't fill the ache inside her soon, she felt like she might explode with frustration.

Then, without torment or teasing, the head of his thick, hard shaft slid easily into her welcoming body, and she mewled at the feeling of being stretched and *full* after so long.

Noah gasped aloud, arching his back as though he was going to leave her.

"No! Please, stay," she begged. She grabbed for him, pressing her heels into his back in encouragement.

"Is it... safe?" Noah whispered, sucking on the flesh of her neck and kissing her ear.

Heat flowed over her, consuming any capability for rational thought. "Of course," she whispered back, bucking her hips up at him in desperation. She was clean. She'd been sure to check after her Ex cheated, and she hadn't been with anyone since. He had no need to fear.

He groaned loudly as he slid his cock back inside her core in one smooth thrust, hitting something unexpected, deep within.

Oh, my God!

She screamed out as her first orgasm crashed through her, surprising the crap out of her and making her cling tightly to his shoulders as if he were a life-preserver in a tumultuous sea. She felt her pussy spasm and ripple, clinging to the man inside of her, welcoming him, thanking him, and rejoicing in him.

"Oh, dear God," Noah groaned and began thrusting faster. He pounded into her again and again, building a wickedly alluring rhythm that her body craved and screamed for.

She bit into his shoulder, tasty hot salty skin and clung to his strong arms as sweat beaded on his back.

Oh God, it's happening again!

With each stroke of his beautiful cock, he stoked the fire in her belly, adding fuel, forcing it to blaze higher and hotter. Again, she cried out for him and gripped him until her nails broke flesh.

Noah's deeply sexy moans grew louder too as he fought a carnal battle with his own body.

Tabitha's second orgasm seized her like a ragdoll and swept her up in a whirlwind of pussy-clenching, Earth-shattering sensations. Bright, pinpricks of light flashed behind her eyelids like a vortex or shooting stars and she whimpered as she weathered the storm of her ecstasy.

Noah's movements became more erratic and jerkier as he powered home *hard*, and then with one final balls-deep thrust, pulses of magnificent warmth filled her like a torrent of heaven. Unwilling to let any of him go to waste, her body proved itself relentless and continued to squeeze and milk Noah until his very last drop was consumed and he was spent.

CHAPTER 11

NOAH

Noah collapsed onto the pillows, the breath rushing out of his lungs in a dramatic *whoosh* as he pulled Tabitha along with him. His orgasm had been so fucking strong, he was still seeing stars. He'd thought he'd be able to maintain control, having enjoyed no foreplay himself. But from the moment Tabitha had come on him just as he'd entered her luscious body, he'd been fighting a losing battle.

And what a magnificent fight to lose!

"That was incredible," he managed to say as his brain did ridiculous cartwheels inside his skull. To be honest, he was amazed he could speak at all after that intense workout. He couldn't even remember the last time he'd had such amazing sex. There was just something about their chemistry that was out of this world. He'd never felt anything like it in the past and that revelation alone made him shake his head in wonder.

This woman is a God-sent.

"*You* were incredible," Tabitha whispered in response as she cuddled into his chest and laid one of her small hands on his flat stomach.

He picked up her hand and examined the short, perfect, clean nails and the soft skin of her palm. Then he brought her hand up to his mouth and kissed it softly, a little part of him wanting to suckle each fingertip and start seducing her all over again. But as willing as his mind was, his body was far too sated to contemplate much beyond that point. So, instead, he laid her hand down once again and let his eyes close with a deep and satisfied sigh.

Shattering his bliss, his phone went off with a tone he recognized as being from the hospital.

Shit.

"Damn. I'm so sorry," he apologized, before he carefully rolled away from her to grab his cell—the one thing he couldn't ignore. "Dr. O'Grady," he answered formally, his brain switching automatically into action mode.

"Doctor, we have Mrs. Phillips in the hospital at the moment and the physician on duty thinks she's experiencing placental abruption."

"Shit. I'll be there in ten minutes," he answered and hung up. He didn't even have time for a shower. With an abruption, depending on the severity of the separation from the wall of the womb, the mother's and baby's life were potentially both in imminent danger; in the very least, the baby's. "I'm *so* sorry, Tabitha," he said as he swiftly pulled a pair of clean pants out of his closet. "One of my patients is going to need a C-section tonight, and I can't in good conscience leave her in the hands of the doctor on duty. She needs me."

Tabitha sat up in bed, pulling the sheet up over herself as her body began to cool in the aftermath of their mind-rocking passion.

"Of course, I totally understand. I'll just get dressed and call for an Uber," she offered without a moment's hesitation. There was no sign of anger or irritation in her expression or voice, which was something he wasn't used to when it came to girlfriends and partners.

"No," he said as he pulled his shirt over his head. He had a very small window of opportunity to get to the hospital in time to save that baby, so he couldn't afford to mess around, but the entire process was relatively swift and efficient if all went well.

"I'll probably be back in a few hours, so if you're happy to just lounge and go to sleep, I'd love for you to stay the night." His stomach filled with butterflies as he preempted her response.

She smiled as she shuffled back so that she could sit up against the headboard. "I don't want to inconvenience you."

He groaned loudly. "Damn, I really do hate this part of my job. I'm so sorry that I have to leave you after that amazing session, but..."

She waved her hand in the air to silence him, her gaze full of warmth and empathy. "*No*, trust me," she said firmly. "I understand. Please, go save your patient. I'll be here when you get back. I promise."

He tugged on his surgical runners and leaned down to kiss her. "Thank you for everything and for being so understanding. We can make up for it by going out for breakfast in the morning, if you like?"

She nodded and smiled contentedly as she nestled back under the covers. "That sounds perfect. I'll see you soon."

Noah grinned and ran out the door to save lives. This was the one part of his life that no girlfriend had *ever* understood. His patients' needs would always come first, because for them it could literally be life or death, and he took his Hippocratic Oath very seriously. He certainly hadn't become a doctor for the fat paycheck. All he'd ever wanted to do was help bring life into the world and make a positive difference.

No amount of money or stress will ever change that.

He took the elevator down to the garage and ran to his car, his mind wandering back to the beautiful woman still snuggled and cozy, naked in his bed. He *really* liked Tabitha. He more than 'liked her' if he was being totally honest with himself. She was different. And the spark that existed between them had fast fanned into a raging inferno he had *no* desire to see extinguished.

He had all his fingers—and toes—crossed that as a nurse, she would have infinitely more patience with his unique and demanding lifestyle than anyone else had. Because after working for twenty long years to get here, he had no intention of letting any of it go. But with any luck, they'd make what they had work around each other's crazy busy schedules.

Afterall, all good relationships were built on a solid foundation of love, trust, understanding, and compromise, weren't they? It was like a long, mutually beneficial game of give and take... or at least, that was what he'd heard. His parents and sisters had been lucky in love, but him? Not so much. But maybe things were destined to turn around for him ... he'd certainly paid his dues.

Or is that just too much to ask?

CHAPTER 12

TABITHA

Noah must have snuck in during the night because when Tabitha woke up after the sun rose, he was nestled in behind her, sound asleep. She lay there for a while, not wanting to wake him up, because she knew the moment she moved, she'd disturb him from his much-needed rest.

I've missed this so much.

It almost pained her to admit. Just waking up with someone close by felt like home. Sleeping alone was horrible, she'd never liked it, even as a child. For Heaven's sake, dogs and cats didn't even like it! They curled up on you and practically slept right up on your head in an effort to be close to you. Close to a beating heart and the comfort of warmth and another living being.

Why are humans the only ones daft enough to live in big houses all alone? And on purpose!

But there was something decidedly different about this morning—excitingly different—about waking up with a man's strong, loving arms around her. Holding her close as if she were someone precious and worthy of being cherished and protected.

Her ex-husband would always stay on his side of the bed, and he had never, not once, reached out to touch her or show affection. But even so, just his breathing pattern had been a small comfort on some deep, primitive level.

But this was intimate and tender and *so* very different to anything she'd ever known. It was wonderful and infinitely better. And she loved it.

"Good morning." Noah voiced invaded her consciousness as groaned and stretched away from her, while keeping a hand on her hip as though losing contact wasn't an option.

"Good morning," she answered. "What time did you get in?" She rolled over to face him and flung a leg over his knee to remain as close as she longed to be.

He rubbed his face and blinked rapidly, trying to wake up properly. "Um, I'm not sure exactly. Three am, I think?"

"Oh, wow, I'm so sorry. You must be exhausted." She'd gotten four whole hours more sleep than him and she could still feel the heavy drag of fatigue on her bones from too many years of arduous shift work.

He grinned that gorgeous smile of his that seemed to promise the world and so much more. "I'll be fine once I wake up in a minute. I slept like a baby once I had you to cuddle."

God, he's beautiful.

She ran her hand over the expanse of his chest, loving every detail of his masculine body that was so different to her own. "Was your patient okay in the end?" she asked, chewing her lower lip.

Given the late hour he'd gotten home, it didn't bode well for the success of his operation. It indicated complications in the very least.

"Hm... yes and no. She'll eventually be okay, I believe. The C-section was much more complicated than normal. Due to the abruption, she lost a lot of blood, but I'll keep a close eye on her over the next few days of her recovery."

She stretched out next to him like a languid, contented cat and checked the time.

Maybe we could fit in another lovemaking session before breakfast?

"Noah, do you think maybe...?"

Then his phone went off again. He reached for it, answering the call with his eyes shut as his free hand pinched the bridge of his nose. "Hm... okay. Yes, you were right to call me. I'll be in soon. Give me half an hour." He groaned as he hung up. "I have to go in early. I hope I can grab a rain check on that breakfast?" he said apologetically.

Disappointment niggled at her mind, but she pushed it away, not allowing it to fester like his girlfriends of the past would have. And she thought *she* worked too much. But poor Noah was on a whole other level compared to her, and she needed to seriously think about whether she wanted a man who was on call twenty-four-seven. She'd never really thought about how it would impact their lives realistically, before now.

She'd been lost to his quick charms and his beautiful smile and had fallen in love with his family before truly assessing the overall situation and what it might mean for their mutual futures. And now, because of her haste, she felt foolish. All of a sudden, Noah's exes didn't seem quite so mad or selfish. Wanting to have your partner's attention and enjoy some uninterrupted quality time with them wasn't a terrible thing, was it?

Shoving that particular train of thought temporarily to the back of her mind, she reached for him and tugged him close, kissing his full lips. "Of course."

"You're a saint," he sighed, before he rolled out of bed, and turned back to hold out his hand. "Want to join me for a quick shower?" he offered. I wish I had time to make love to you again, but we'll have to wait for another day."

"Sounds great," she said as she jumped up and joined him in his huge, luxurious shower, loving the fun and laughter he naturally injected into everything they did together. And as they scrubbed up, she only wished she had time to explore his beautiful body the way she wanted to.

Before long he headed back to the hospital, and she took an Uber home.

Ridiculously, she missed him already and a gray cloud followed her the entire drive. Did she really want someone who would always put her second? Who literally jumped to attention like a paratrooper the moment his cell rang?

Am I being extremely selfish expecting to be put first when the man is quite literally saving lives?

As a nurse, she knew exactly how important a physician's job was—they were literally the final frontier between life and death.

Probably.

The doubts and worries whirled around in her mind until she was a blithering mass of confusion. Was there even room in his life for her? How did anyone with that much riding on their time and skills find happiness? She had no idea, and the lack of available answers was beginning to frustrate her.

There was only one way to work all of this out, and that was by talking to her sister. Sam always fixed everything. "Change of plans!" she called out to her Uber driver. "Can you take me to one twenty-one Fenacre Circle? Thanks."

CHAPTER 13

TABITHA

Tabitha was soon sitting in her sister's kitchen, while Sam attempted to rearrange her entire pantry.

"I don't know if this is normal or not. I know they call it nesting, but I feel the need to organize *everything*. I started with John's tie collection yesterday and ended up doing the whole walk-in closet, our bathroom, and now the kitchen feels like an utter mess."

Tabitha laughed. "I have no idea if it's normal or not, Sam. I've never had the pleasure of going through nesting before."

Her sister continued to pull jars out and rearrange them, while looking over her shoulder at Tabitha with her brow quirked. "So?

How'd your date go last night? Am I correct in assuming you haven't been home yet? You're still wearing my clothes," she observed with an all-too-knowing smile.

Tabitha glanced down at her wrinkled black pencil skirt. "Yeah, I was on my way home this morning, but detoured to you."

"Because?" Sam asked while continuing to sort and wipe down her kitchen like a woman possessed, or very heavily pregnant with twins.

How do I put this?

Tabitha opened her mouth, then when nothing came out, she shut it again. She may as well just spill it out. There really was no pretty or elegant way to give voice to the thoughts swirling in her mind. She sighed and began. "Well, because I'm starting to think that we just don't suit."

"Argh!" Her sister groaned out loud, spinning to face her with her hands clenched into fists of frustration. "I *knew* you'd do this. The moment he showed you he was a decent human being you could actually fall in love with, you'd find something wrong with him and get cold feet."

Well, that isn't fair.

"Oh, no, that's not it, Sam."

Her sister's glare clearly indicated that she didn't believe her.

Tabitha sighed heavily. Hiding anything from her sister was fruitless, but that didn't mean she was necessarily correct. "Look, you're right about one thing. Noah is amazing. He's funny, happy, and attentive. He even took me to meet his family last night, and they were all great, too."

That got her sister's attention. Sam stopped what she was doing, and her eyes grew wide, her eyebrows almost high enough to reach her hairline. "Really? What was that like?"

Tabitha sighed again, this time with residual happiness as the memories returned to her. "It was out-of-a-movie-perfect, actually.

It was his nephew's birthday, so the whole family was there. It was super casual, with lots of food, drinks, cake etc."

Her sister rolled her eyes and clucked her tongue. "You *know* that's not what I mean, Tabitha."

"Oh, yeah, sorry. His family adores him and only wants what's best for him. They were all friendly, but his sisters pushed me a bit, so I pushed back, and they seemed happy with what I had to say." That was something she loved about the O'Grady women. What conversations they could have in another life!

Sam grabbed a bottle of water from the fridge and poured them each a glass. "And what was Dr. O'Grady like... you know, with the other kids, and his parents, and stuff? I find it hard to imagine him as anything other than a professional, well-dressed doctor."

Tabitha pursed her lips together, allowing herself time to think about the question properly. "He was great; really friendly, happy, and affectionate. His niece and nephews kept jumping into his arms, so we barely had a moment to talk, but it all felt so..."

"So?"

She reached for the words. "So... normal and natural. Like we'd done it all a hundred times before." And that really was the key to the success of the day. She hadn't felt awkward or unwanted. Noah hadn't made her serve him or run around trying to make everyone like her. He'd just left her to stand on her own two feet to find her bearings, and she appreciated and respected that about him.

"So, then... what's the problem, Sis?" Sam asked skeptically.

She didn't want to answer her sister's question. She really didn't. It flew in the face of everything she'd ever thought of herself or voiced to others. And she was ashamed.

"Come on, Tabitha. I know there's something. You know you can tell me anything, right?"

Tabitha tapped her palm on her forehead. Honesty was the best way to go.

Well, here goes...

"It's his job," she admitted with a heavy heart.

Her sister who had returned to scrubbing her kitchen, stopped cleaning the sink—not a good sign—and gave Tabitha her full and undivided attention. "What do you mean, it's his job? Because if you think he's not competent, you need to speak to some of his patients. I know I haven't gone through the actual labor yet, but he's been the perfect obstetrician for me so far."

Tabitha waved her hands in and out in a 'no way' gesture. "Oh, no, it's not that. I know he's a great doctor. I can see it in the way he treats his staff, his epic wait list of private patients, his manner, and well, everything." Her professional personality could spot a good doctor at a hundred paces.

"I don't understand. Then what's the problem?" Sam asked for the second time as if she'd garnered no clarity at all from Tabitha's admission.

And too late she realized that this wasn't the sort of thing she could confide to her sister about. After all, her husband John worked ridiculous hours and Sam never complained. She probably liked it, though. Some women did. It meant more free time and certainly more family money to spend.

Tabitha waved her hand again to dismiss the conversation. "Never mind. I'll figure it out."

"Oh, don't give me that crap, Tabby Cat! Come on." Sam beckoned to her. "Just tell me already."

"You're going to think I'm stupid."

Sam grinned with the confidence of a true sister. "Yeah... *and?*" She was right. Sam had seen her at every high and every heartbreakingly stupid low. If anyone could figure out the mess of a human she was, it really was her sister.

With a defeated sigh Tabitha gave up. It was high time she put her pride aside and see if her concerns had any basis in reality or not. "Okay. Honestly, I'm not sure I want to be with someone who is on call fifty weeks a year, twenty-four hours a day. I mean... we barely made it through sex last night and he was running back to the hospital. And then this morning we were meant to do breakfast and he got called back again."

Her sister's whole posture relaxed, and she began to chuckle as she shook her head.

"Oh, goodness, is that all, Tabby? Really? Of course, you're worried about that!"

Relief flooded through Tabitha at her sister's immediate understanding.

"So, you get it?" she asked hesitantly once her sister's laughter died down.

"Yes, of course. Even with men who aren't physicians, like John for example, there are always sacrifices to be made for them to hold fantastic jobs where they make good money." Sam abandoned her washcloth in the sink and came to sit down beside her.

"For you, it's going to mean that he'll always be late, forever leaving early, and rarely have any vacation time. But at least you'll always know where he is. He'd be at the hospital, potentially saving lives and making a real difference in this world. For me, it means we have to move around a lot, and John's lucky if he's home before nine at night—and then he's gone again by the time I wake up in the morning. But I consider what I have a great life. And I John and everything he does for us. So, I make do with the cards we are dealt. You just need to decide if Noah's worth the loneliness. If all the perks and joys of being with him outweigh the negatives."

It sounded like Sam made some real sacrifices. She never really saw just how brave, independent, and flexible her younger sister truly was. And she'd certainly never given her enough credit for it. "How do you do it then, Sam?" she asked.

Samantha shrugged, a soft smile playing across her lips and lighting up her pretty face despite the shadows under her eyes.

"It's easy, really. You just need to fill up your day and your life with other things. Unfortunately, your husband, or whatever he happens to be, can't be the center of your world. It rarely works like that, and to be honest, it's not that healthy to be so wholly dependent on someone like that. It's good to find a balance whether you enjoy each other's company, but don't need it to survive. So, whether he's there or not, your life needs to go on. You can keep working full-time if that helps, or volunteer at the hospital. Maybe go on holidays with girlfriends, or come visit me every weekend? Or just simply enjoy the peace, before babies come along and ruin all of that!" Sam laughed but rubbed her belly with obvious affection.

A lightbulb lit up in her mind and understanding like she'd never felt before suddenly dawned upon her. "Is that why you're so excited about the twins, Sam? Company?"

"Yeah, in a way," she admitted with hesitation. "They'll certainly keep me busy, although we've already talked about perhaps hiring a live-in nanny to help me, especially for the first year. As John won't be able to do the nightly feeds or help me walk the hallways with screaming babies at night if he's working eighty-hour weeks to keep us afloat." Her sister heaved a heavy sigh.

Tabitha's heart twinged with guilt and longing. "That's a good idea, Sam. It sounds like you could use the support. I just wish I could come with you and help you."

Samantha smiled poignantly. "You've got your own life to live, and I'm grateful for that—for you. I only want you to be happy, Tabitha. You need to know that. I love you *so* much."

Tabitha reached out and grabbed her sister's hand, squeezing it tightly. "I love you too, Sam."

"Please, sweetheart, be happy," were her sister's final words to her for the day.

Tabitha left her sister's house feeling lighter and happier than she had in ages. She'd told herself to follow her instincts about Noah, especially after having sex with him for the first time, and that's exactly what she would seriously do.

Making love to Noah had proven what an incredibly giving and passionate person he was. He was the very definitely of selfless and loving. He was worth investing her heart in, she just knew it. Maybe the tide had finally turned for her and karma was finally giving her what she deserved after so much heartache.

Because there was a long while there where she'd been unsure of *everything* in her world. And it felt more than good to feel the steadiness of the ground beneath her feet once more.

CHAPTER 14

NOAH

Noah finished a fifteen-hour shift and fell into bed, his exhaustion intensified by the lack of sleep from the night before and the massive orgasm that had drained of him of practically all his testosterone. But what a night it had been. Tabitha had been everything he'd ever wanted in a lover—passionate, honest and one of the rare beauties capable of multiple orgasms! He fell asleep with a smile on his face and content heart.

The following morning, with the sun shining through his curtains, he woke to a dozen messages on his phone. Some from his sisters, a few from the hospital, and one from his beautiful nurse-girlfriend. He liked the sound of 'girlfriend' and already craved to make their relationship more official with titles, but his gorgeous woman had seemed hesitant to put labels on anything just yet. He completely understood, given the speed and short nature of their union thus far and the pains of her past, but he had no intention of letting her go and wanted to share how he felt with the whole world. He sighed deeply.

Tabitha.

As he lay in bed, staring up at the shadows stretching across the ceiling, slowly stroking his cock, he let the memories of their time together flow over him.

Then his phone went off with the hospital's familiar ringtone.

"Argh... At least I got to sleep in." He answered the phone and rolled out of bed. It was time to go back to what he did best: delivering babies and christening new parents.

By the end of his shift, his need to see Tabitha again had grown. Every time he saw a nurse stick her head in the surgical suite, or his consulting room, he hoped it was her. Which was ridiculous given she didn't work in the same hospital. All the same, he was beginning to think that he'd have to ask her to come work with him soon, or he'd never be able to get his mind back on track.

He picked up the phone and called her, but it went straight through to voicemail. She was obviously working. Instead of leaving a message, he hung up and texted her, asking her to call back whenever she had time. They just *had* to set up another dinner, or lunch, or even a sleepover. If they didn't, he'd surely go mad. The very thought of her was intoxicating and he couldn't wait to kiss those beautiful, soft lips again.

Heading home alone, he was welcomed by the eerie quiet of his condo—and it felt wrong. For the first time in a long time, he wished he had a woman to greet him when he came home. And not just any woman. He wanted Tabitha.

But she wasn't here, and he had only his thoughts to keep him company, so he called in a Grubhub order and got some Thai delivered. It was delicious, but eating alone no longer held the appeal it once did. Even on the days he was tired enough to consider himself a walking zombie, he still yearned for Tabitha's presence.

Tabitha called him back when he was at work the next day, and he wasn't able to get back to her until Monday night. They played phone tag for days, until finally he managed to hear her voice in real time—and it was heavenly.

"Hello, stranger! Long time, no see," Noah said down the line, unable to hide the excited smile from his voice.

She laughed, the sound like music to his ears. "I know. Ugh. These shifts are going to be a *major* problem for us in future. We're going to need to schedule our dates a week in advance!"

He grinned against the phone, though a strange tug unexpectedly pulled from within his stomach. "We just might," he answered. A protracted silence followed, and he realized they didn't yet know enough about each other to charge forth into that conversation. But it was nice to know she was even thinking about the future. It meant she saw legitimate potential in their relationship too.

"Ah... so, what are your plans for Christmas this year?" he asked in an attempt to shatter the quiet that had fallen between them.

She groaned in a frustrated way. "Oh, God, don't ask."

He sat down on his couch and got comfortable. It seemed as though he'd found a topic they could have a real conversation about. "Don't tell me you're not obsessed by Christmas like every other woman I know. How long have you had your tree up already? A month?" He relaxed and grinned anew as he prodded for information. It was only the fifth of December, but those who really loved Christmas and got into the spirit of the season threw themselves into their decorating very early. They always did.

"Argh," she protested. "As if! I had *no* intention of putting it up at all, but now I have to."

"You just got more interesting, Tabitha. Don't tell me you don't like Christmas?"

"Don't tell me you do?" she scoffed back.

He chuckled and glanced around his bare apartment. There was not a single sprig of holly or a red shiny bauble anywhere to be found, and there never would be. "Not in the least," he agreed.

She sighed. "Oh, thank goodness. I wasn't sure I could deal with a man who thought Christmas was all magical and crap. It's bad enough my mum and sister are all gaga over it."

"Well, you don't have to worry about that. This guy right here is quite happy to work all Christmas Day, New Years, and Easter. There's no rest for the wicked, as they say!" Another bout of silence ensued and it made him wonder.

Did I say something?

"Ah, what wrong?"

"Um... it's nothing. I just— no, you're right."

"Don't you work through the holidays, too?" he asked her.

Surely, she didoes?

"Yes... usually, but I took Christmas off this year, as I'm hosting for my sister. Sam's far too pregnant to be putting so much stress on herself at this point."

"Oh, that's good to hear. You're a great sister, Tabitha. Samantha's lucky to have someone like you looking out for her."

"Yes... um, I guess. Anyway, I better go. I just finished a double shift, so I'm going to get something to eat and some sleep while I can."

Noah stood up, nervous energy zinging through his bloodstream.

Shit. What's going on?

Her entire demeanor had changed in a heartbeat, and it made him feel anxious in a decidedly uncomfortable way.

"Can we book in our next date? What day works for you?"

"Um..." Tabitha mumbled with a lack of commitment or enthusiasm.

"Tomorrow?" he prompted hopefully. More silence hung between them, and he wondered where he'd gone wrong. They'd been getting along so well for a moment there, and he thought they'd bonded over their mutual lack of love for Christmas. He grimaced, hanging on tenterhooks as he awaited her answer.

"Ah, I..."

"I apologize if I said something wrong, Tabitha," he interjected when it seemed she would be no more forthcoming. "I didn't mean anything by the Christmas comments. I'm just not really into the holiday thing."

"No, it's not that. It's just that..."

"What? What's wrong?" he pressed. "You can talk to me Tabitha. With our schedules we're only going to be able to move forward with an open line of communication." His brain raced over everything he'd said, and he still couldn't pinpoint his error.

What gave her cold feet all of a sudden?

"I'm not working tomorrow," she offered, dodging his line of questioning. "We could meet for lunch, or something?"

He had appointments on and off all day long, but he could work something out. For her, he'd move mountains. "Perfect. Do you mind if I message you tomorrow with a time when I know where' I'm at?"

"Yeah, no problem. Bye for now," she said, and the call ended.

She'd sounded strangely sad, and he hung up the phone scratching his head, his brows knitted in consternation. Sure, their timetables were going to clash, and he was sure they'd struggle to find time together, but didn't shift workers do this all the time? It wasn't like she'd come into this relationship blind. She had to know what she was getting herself into... She was a nurse, and he was a doctor, it was always going to be a matter of juggling their lives and trying to keep all their respective balls in the air as they went. But if they had a real connection, wasn't that worth working for?

Heaving a troubled sigh, Noah went about his day with a strange, unsettled feeling niggling at his gut, like his new relationship was on the downward slope and fast plummeting into oblivion... like so many had before. And despite his natural sense of resilience built up over years of long hours and hard work, he felt distinctly disappointed. A lot more than he expected himself to be, and it hurt more than he dared to admit.

CHAPTER 15

TABITHA

Tabitha glanced up at the mistletoe hanging over her front door. Her sister had strung it up there last night, and although she'd didn't love it, she certainly didn't hate it either.

Noah's blasé comments about working through *every* holiday had really hit a sour spot inside of her.

Sure, she considered the holidays a shameful waste of money, and a whole lot of pomp for nothing, generally speaking... but she'd do anything to be with her sister on Christmas Day. And if that meant working every weekend for two months beforehand, then she'd do it without a second thought. She didn't have a big family, but what she did have was important to her—they always had been.

Noah's familiar and expensive bachelor's car pulled up at her curb, derailing her train of thought, and she grabbed her keys and headed out the door.

He got out to greet her like a gentleman, a smile on his face as he opened and shut the passenger side door for her.

She appreciated the noble gesture, so she smiled in return as she settled into his car. But the feeling, as she had expected, was off, almost strained.

"Hey, you. It's so good to see you," Noah said as he hovered over the center console and reached for her with both hands, his gaze so intensely genuine that it punched her in the gut *hard.*

She let him cup her face and draw her closer, falling into his kiss like she'd promised herself she would. This man was a doctor, a surgeon, and a true healer. He was professional and empathetic, beloved by his colleagues and patients alike. Not to mention he was a generous and amazing lover. Whatever little problems she was allowing to fester her hopes for a future together could surely be overcome?

We just need to communicate, like he said.

When he pulled back, she smiled brightly, determined not to self-sabotage. "And how's your week been?" she prompted. Work was safe territory when it came to conversation at least.

"Oh, good. Busy, as always. Never a dull moment, really. You?"

"Um..." she smiled at the fact he'd asked her a reciprocal question. Her ex-husband had never, not in an entire year of living with him, had he ever thought to ask her how her day was. He simply avoided the question—because he hadn't cared. "The same. The E.R. is a little quiet now, but we all know it will be simply *crazy* over Christmas and New Year period, so not necessarily looking forward to that. But it is what it is."

Noah groaned as he pulled the car onto the road, and they drove them out of her street. "Oh, God, yes! I remember those shifts during my residency. The E.R. was complete insanity over Christmas. You're not working that day, this year, though, right?"

"No, not this year," she confirmed. "But New Year's often worse. There's just so much alcohol-fueled stupidity."

Noah smiled—obviously reliving the memories of when those sorts of days were his problem—but didn't say anything.

She laughed and shook her head. "I suppose your world's pretty far away from that, now, huh?"

He grinned. "Oh, definitely. The worst thing I have to deal with on Christmas Day is women going into labor, just like every other day."

"So, it's no different for you, I suppose." She swallowed hard against the uncomfortable knot rubbing in her throat.

Stay calm, Tabitha. Just talk it out. Don't be stupid.

Noah's hand came over to rest on her thigh and squeezed. "Hey. I thought you and I agreed on the fact that Christmas was a whole lot of stress for no good reason?"

"We did... I mean, we do. I agree with you."

"But...?" he pressed, clearly unwilling to let matters remain unresolved.

She looked down at her hands where they were playing with the pattern on her leggings. "But... I don't work on Christmas if I can help it. I like being with my family. And I know I bitch and moan about the money and the effort, but my family's important to me."

"So is mine," he answered. "You've seen that."

That's true.

The time she'd spent with his family was casual, peaceful, and beautiful. There was real warmth and love there. "I know I have... I suppose your comment about being happy to work right through all the holidays just got to me a bit. That's all, I'm sorry."

Noah pulled up outside a cute little local café that she'd always wanted to eat at but had never gotten the time or chance to.

"Oh, great," she said, shoving her anxiety down. "I've heard this place is really nice."

Noah smiled. "Let's go in, then." He jumped out of the car and opened the door for her.

She followed suit and climbed out, keeping an eye on the time as she was pretty sure he'd need to get back before too long. "What time do you need to return to the hospital?" she asked, just to be safe.

"Not for another hour or so. We've got heaps of time."

That didn't seem like a lot, but she knew what it was like with shift work, and ten-minute breaks felt like a lifetime when you'd barely stopped to breathe in hours.

They got settled into a booth and quickly ordered.

Tabitha opened her mouth to start a normal conversation but found the Christmas issue was still paramount on her mind. "So, where is Christmas Day for you when you do manage it? Your mom's house?"

Noah nodded as he picked up his foamy latte. "Yeah, it always is. My sisters fight her every year to have it at their places, but Mom always wins that battle. She's the matriarch, plus, her house is the biggest by far, so it accommodates everyone much better."

"Her house definitely seems great for parties. I'd wondered at first why your nephew's birthday party was at your mom's, rather than your sisters."

He shrugged. "It's just her way—her love language. As long as she's well enough to do it, she'll have a hundred parties a year at her place for us. She's the hostess with the mostest," he joked.

Tabitha smiled to herself as she placed a powdered pink marshmallow into her hot chocolate, love swelling in her chest to replace her lingering doubts. "I like that," she said simply. A dominant, loving matriarch would make for a happy and well-cared-for family, that was for sure.

"So, you said you're doing Christmas at your place this year?" Noah asked.

"Yeah, it wasn't my original plan. I believe I have you to thank for that," she said cocking an eyebrow and smirking playfully.

His eyebrows flew up on his forehead. "Um, me? How come?"

She laughed. "I think it was you who told my sister not to stress about Christmas at her house, so she foisted it off onto me."

He chuckled loudly, almost losing his mouthful of coffee. "That would be right! My own good advice coming back to smack me in the face."

"It was the best advice for her. I was pleased when she asked me, because I knew it meant that she could have the day to rest, and God knows she needs it."

"Or give birth," he reminded her.

Their meals arrived and Tabitha picked up her crisp, warm focaccia. "This looks amazing," she gushed and bit into her flavorful lunch.

"I agree." Noah picked up his own lunch when his phone went off, with that same familiar ringtone she'd heard too many times already now.

"Is that the hospital?" she asked, her gut sinking despite her best efforts to keep her mood bright.

"Yeah." He took his cell out of his pocket and answered. "Dr. O'Grady. Yes... Yes... okay. I'll be there in five minutes." He hung up and looked at her with that same regretful expression she'd seen days ago. "Tabitha, I'm so sorry, I need to go." He pulled some money out of his wallet and called the waiter over. "Here, this is for the meal, and would you mind wrapping mine up for takeout, please. I have an emergency to attend."

The waiter rushed away with his order.

Noah began to pack up, picking up his keys and his jacket. "I can drop you back at your house quickly, if you want?" His energy had changed to one of business and efficiency.

The waiter returned promptly and delivered his wrapped lunch to him in a cardboard box. "Your meal, sir."

Meanwhile, hers still sat temptingly on her plate. Tabitha shook her head. "No, I'm all good, thanks. I think I'll take my time and walk home. It's only a few blocks away."

"Are you sure... because..."

She waved her hand dismissively. "It's my day off, so I'm going to relax. Go, please. But call me later?"

"Thanks, beautiful. I will." Noah ducked his head to kiss her.

She lifted her chin gladly to receive the kiss as memories of their night together flowed over her, the weight of her decision momentarily lifted.

Too soon he flew out the door, climbed into his fancy car and was gone.

Tabitha lifted her hot chocolate to her lips and took a long drink, savoring the sweetness. This was what her life was going to be like if they stayed together. He was married to his job and she would always be the mistress begging for scraps of his time.

She ate her lunch in peace and squashed the negative feelings in her mind. Even as she walked home, the threatening black clouds hanging overhead didn't alter her strange mood. There was a numbness blossoming inside her mind and she wasn't sure how to break through it successfully.

There was a strange sense of inevitability settling over her that she couldn't fight. It felt like she was being swallowed by quicksand, and no matter how hard she struggled, she couldn't break free. This wasn't the life she wanted for herself. To be moved aside in favor of her man's work, every single day.

And she knew with a soul-crushing clarity that the best way to avoid that would be to become a beck-and-call wife. If she quit her job and stayed home, no matter what tiny fragments of time he could give her, she'd be there and ready to receive them. But that wasn't her, not now, and never would be. She deserved more from life, and she'd never throw away her career. She's worked too long and too hard. Being able to support herself and remain self-reliant was important to her, especially after the divorce.

No way. That's not happening. I'm going to stand on my own two feet, even if the price of that freedom is pain.

She walked the long way home, her thoughts a jumble of emotion and heart-wrenching apathy. By the time she reached her house her fingers were freezing cold. Stripping, she stepped into the bathroom and took a long shower. Afterward, she did some laundry and busied herself about the place as she waited for the phone call that would seal it all.

CHAPTER 16

NOAH

Noah glanced at the clock and hid away in his office. He had a ten-minute break and needed it to get in touch with Tabitha. His conscience was eating away at him for abandoning her in the café today. That was low, even for him. He'd realized afterward that he hadn't even asked if she'd wanted hers wrapped up too; because his brain had already transported itself to the hospital, ready to perform the C-section he knew was necessary for his patient.

He plucked out his cell and noted there were no messages from her. If nothing else, Tabitha certainly wasn't a clingy girlfriend. If that was what she was. They hadn't gotten to discuss the level of their relationship just yet, largely due to the interruptions his work presented. He sighed and tapped in her number. The phone rang twice before she picked it up.

"Hey, Noah. Did you finish your shift already?"

Her tone sounded optimistic, so he was annoyed to have to tell her the truth. "No, I'm just on break at the moment and thought I'd call."

"Oh, thanks."

And the mood shifted as simply as that. "How was the rest of your afternoon?" he asked, attempting to salvage the call.

"It was great, thanks. I enjoy peaceful days to myself. I rarely get them while having to pick up so many extra shifts at work. I'm sure you can empathize."

He chuckled awkwardly. "Ah, yeah. I certainly can. Sleep is usually my main priority when I get home."

"Yeah... speaking of which, I really need to get a few hours' sleep before my night shift starts, so I better go, Noah."

"Hang on, can we schedule another date sometime soon? I know you're about to get extremely busy, but I'm sure we can slip in a coffee date, or something?"

"You mean like today?" Her tone altered slightly, like the wind changed unexpectedly and brought with it an arctic front.

He shivered and grimaced, sucking in a deep breath. "Well today was unusual..."

"Was it?" she asked before he'd even had a chance to speak. "Is it unusual for you to have to leave at a moment's notice for a patient?"

He didn't like where this was going or her tone. She was leading them down a dangerous path and she knew it. His stomach lurched. "Well... no, it's not," admitted. "But usually, I can grab another hour or so, as you know from last week."

"Well, Noah," she said with a sigh. "I'll be honest with you. I don't think I can keep going on dates where I'm left behind the moment work beckons. And that's assuming we can even find the time to see each other in the first place."

That sounds like an ultimatum. Please, please don't be like the rest.

"Tabitha, what are you saying?" he asked carefully, keeping his own tone as neutral as possible.

"I'm saying that I don't think this isn't going to work, Noah. As much as a part of me wants this, it seems your life and mine simply don't fit together."

"That's probably true to a certain degree," he said. "But if you were to work here, we could co-ordinate shifts. We could get more time; we'd know each other's schedules in advance."

She laughed without humor. "Me, change my job? Why should it be my position that has to give, Noah?" she asked. "Why don't you tell your patients that you'll only see them during your scheduled shifts and won't be on call twenty-four-seven? There *are* other obstetric doctors—very good ones too—available when you're not rostered on."

He hissed in a breath. What she was suggesting was totally against his personal philosophy on medicine. When he took on a client it meant he'd decided very consciously and purposely to be there for them no matter what. And babies rarely liked to stick to schedules. "That's not possible, Tabitha. You know that."

"It is for every single other specialty except yours," she replied with stone-cold calm. "And *you* know you could take on a partner, one who could share the workload and take on all your cases when you're not at the hospital."

He ground his teeth together and pursed his lips. Yes, he could technically do that. Plenty of specialists tag-teamed in such a manner. But he'd never found a doctor he trusted with his patients as much as he trusted himself. And that was a hard thing to find. It's why he was still practicing solo. "I could. That's true," he had to agree.

"But you don't want to change anything about your life, do you, Noah? Because work is your number-one priority, and no woman, no matter how much you like her, is ever going to come even a close second in your life, is she?"

Noah groaned and ran a hand through his hair in frustration. "Oh, give me a break, Tabitha, please. You, of all people, should understand my line of work. I thought as a nurse you would be more empathetic than this. Your schedule is almost as hectic as mine," he reasoned.

How could I have been so wrong again?

This was why he'd stopped dating in the first place. It was precisely why he'd given up on the hopes of ever having a wife and children, like everyone else. It was just too difficult. It seemed an impossible dream, far from his reach. No woman he'd ever met was willing to meet his level of sacrifice with their own.

"Empathetic? Are you serious? I'm a nurse for God's sake. That's a low blow, Noah. Empathy and compassion *are* my business, but I don't think my requests are that unreasonable. Do you?"

"Requests? You haven't even made any requests yet. You've just got complaints." He pinched the bridge of his nose as he heard her sigh.

Shit. This is going downhill real fast.

"You're right. Well, Noah, my request is that you find a way to have a simple lunch date with me once a week without being called away. Do you think you could find a way to make that possible?"

"Is that it?" he asked, his brow furrowed. Because that sounded entirely too reasonable.

"Well... Yes. But I suppose it's really more a symptom of a bigger issue."

Oh, here it comes.

"Yes, perhaps. But what do you mean, specifically?"

"It's ah... my fear, more than anything else," she admitted, her tone a little more vulnerable and less abrasive.

Noah ground his teeth together and tried not to groan aloud. He had all the patience in the world for women when they were in labor, but when all they wanted to do was point out his failings, his patience had its limits. "And what's that?"

"It's that *if* we stay together, we'll never have a proper life together. That we'll never fit in any vacations, and you'll be running off in the middle of every dinner, birthday party... or Christmas," she finished, her voice trailing off.

Anger bubbled up inside him almost instantly and he felt helpless to control it. This was the same exact crap gift-wrapped with a different name tag! He'd heard it a hundred times before, and it made him want to bang his head against a fucking wall. This wasn't about scheduling or compatibility at all!

"This is all about *Christmas*, isn't it? I should have known you were too good. to be true. Finding a woman who doesn't go crazy about Christmas is like finding a needle in a haystack." He sighed. "Listen, Tabitha, I think you may be right. It seems we don't suit after all. I just can't deal with that."

Her tone turned to ice once more. "Yeah, I am right. You have your work, and I have mine. I couldn't give up my shift work, even if I wanted to, so asking you to change is totally unfair."

"Um..."

Maybe I was a bit harsh?

"Thanks, Noah, for everything."

And Tabitha hung up before he could get the words together. Sadness flowed over him, stronger than he'd expected. He'd lost her.

She's done.

His personal receptionist poked her head in the door. "Dr. O'Grady? Your next appointment is here, now."

"Oh, thanks, Cheryl. Please, show her in," he answered automatically.

He went about his day as he always did, but there was a sense of overwhelming moroseness that he couldn't quash. He'd really thought Tabitha would be someone special to him. That she would fit into his life where no one else had. He'd really believed they stood a chance. Their chemistry was off the starts, she worked in the same industry and so understood his work commitments, and she'd also won his family over in no time flat.

But once again he was wrong, and it seemed that he was destined to be alone forever. And the saddest part of all was the realization that Tabitha might have been right in more ways than one. Perhaps he was the reason for his own misery and that was a hard pill to swallow, indeed.

CHAPTER 17

TABITHA

"Are you sure you don't need any more money for Christmas dinner? Have you got everything?" her younger sister asked over the phone.

Tabitha glanced at her over-stocked fridge and over-flowing pantry. "Yeah, Sam. I've got everything. There's enough stuff here to sink a battleship and then some." She'd made a concerted effort to keep herself busy, shopping for Christmas and decorating the house with all the fun and festive Christmas decorations her sister had purchased. The whole house kind of looked like the elves went to town on it.

"How are you doing, anyway, sis? You know, with the Noah thing?"

A pain stabbed at Tabitha's ribs, but she mentally pushed it away, unwilling to give it her time or energy. "What Noah thing, Sam? We went on maybe two dates and had sex once. That isn't exactly a long-term relationship."

"I know... but..."

"No buts, Sam. You'll be seeing Noah more than me now. And speaking of doctors, how are those gorgeous babies doing?" Despite her sadness and turmoil over her break-up with Noah, she'd convinced Sam to continue seeing him. She'd initially wanted to abandon him and find a new doctor in sisterly solidarity, but Tabitha had squashed that idea quick smart. Noah, after all, was a brilliant physician. It was because of his commitment to his patients that she'd broken up with him... sort of.

She still couldn't decide if she'd been the one to officially call it off in the end, or if he had. Because she was pretty sure he'd trumped her by the end of the conversation, but she'd given voice to the issues bothering her and said what she'd had to say and that was the end of it.

"Oh, they're huge. I can barely do anything now! But John's been helping me with everything, and I've had Grubhub deliver practically every day this week, because cooking in my state is totally not happening."

Tabitha smiled. John would spare no expense or effort when it came to looking after her sister and it melted her heart. "He's a good man, Sam. I'm glad he takes care of you so well. You deserve it."

"Oh, that he is," she agreed readily. "And Mom's been by and cleaned the whole house from top to bottom for me, too, in preparation of the twins' arrival."

"That was good of her. I'll be over after my shift today if you have some washing for me to do or..."

Sam laughed, her tone relaxed and full of light. "You're so much like Mom, Tabby. That would be great, thank you so much, hon. I'll see you soon."

They hung up together and Tabitha glanced at her cell, where a silent vibrating alarm was going off on one of her apps. She frowned down at it. It was her period app.

That's odd. The damn thing had skipped her mind entirely. She clicked on the notification and saw the message clear as day. Her period was officially almost a week late.

Impossible.

She clicked back to last month's calendar and checked over her dates again. She'd used the app since before she got married and had hoped to use it to work out her fertility windows for when they tried to get pregnant, but instead when they'd divorced, she'd simply ended up using it to track her cycle. It was normally like clockwork.

It's not like she was on any sort of contraception or medication that might be messing with her, so that explanation was out the door. So, why should she be late? She wasn't having sex with anyone...

"Oh—holy shit!" Her hand flew to her mouth, blocking the second stream of obscenities that flowed like water from a faucet. In a flurry of panic she scrolled back and counted.

Yes, a week late.

Or... five days. That wasn't too bad, although she was *never* late. Not even by half a day. Her menses arrived first thing in the morning every time she was due. Ridiculously, her period was one of the most reliable damn things in her life. Her heart began to pound, and a sickening feeling worked its way into her gut like a worm burrowing through soil.

She checked her diary and took note of the date of her night with Noah, then flicked back to her period app. Day twelve. It literally fell within the sixteen-to-thirty-two-hour window of ovulation.

Oh, shit. The worst possible day.

But what were the chances, really? She bit into her bottom lip. Too many of her friends had a history of trouble conceiving. Especially where stress was involved. It could take months, years even. Cortisol worked havoc on your system, and she, for one, was always stressed with her chaotic shift work. Surely, she couldn't be pregnant after one night? One time? And he'd used protection. Hadn't he? He was a doctor for fuck's sake, he wouldn't have neglected such an important thing.

She wracked her memory, running a hand through her long blonde hair and recalled him asking her something about her being safe... "Oh, no."

He hadn't been asking about diseases, he'd been asking about *protection*. He'd probably wanted to know if she was on the pill or had an IUD. But at that point in time, it had been the farthest thing from her mind She'd been married—the last thing she'd been worried about was a condom, or having to be on the pill, just 'in case' of a one-night-stand. Because she didn't do those!

Oh shit, he's going to blame me for this... and he probably should.

"Calm, down. Don't get ahead of yourself," she muttered to herself, taking a few deep, steadying breaths. There was still no guarantee she was ever pregnant, yet. Her body could just be having a bit of a hissy fit. She'd certainly been through the ringer, lately. She could easily grab a test from work tonight and do it when she went to the toilet.

No big deal.

It was still definitely possible that she was just late. It wouldn't be the first time stress had provoked an unusual cycle in a woman. She was a nurse and knew shit like this happened all the time. It'd just never happened to her, personally.

It's going to be fine. It is. Just fine.

The day passed so slowly she found herself grinding her teeth and glancing at the clock more than usual. And by the time her night shift finally started, Tabitha was chewing on her nails in an attempt to deal with her ramped-up anxiety. She'd already looked at the scenario in every which way, and she didn't even know if it was true or not and the feeling of not knowing was eating her alive. She *needed* to find out if she was, indeed, pregnant or not, and deal with the repercussions.

She grabbed a test kit from one of the storeroom shelves, tucked it into the pocket of her scrubs and practically bolted to the bathroom. Sitting on the toilet was one of the craziest experiences of her life. Holding the strip beneath herself, and peeing on the absorbent tip while trying not to get it all over her hands. Even as a nurse, she wasn't a natural. Her panic made her hands shake.

She slid the tip back on and placed it on top of the toilet paper roll as she cleaned herself up and got re-dressed. The instruction leaflet said to wait three minutes, but she could already see the line beginning to form.

One line—yes!

That meant she wasn't... and then that dreaded second line began to stand out against the stark white background, her heart fell.

No... this isn't the way it's supposed to go!

She was pregnant at Christmas by a man who didn't even want her. A man who wouldn't even try to be flexible enough to pursue a relationship with her. He'd deemed her unworthy of such an effort.

Fuck it.

She put the toilet seat down and collapsed onto it, holding the stick in her hand as the lines got bluer and bluer. Clearer and clearer. Among the chaos in her mind, as a nurse, she realized that she should probably have a blood test to confirm., But her lack of a period, and this obviously very positive affirmation were proof enough for her.

She rubbed her fingers against her temples, fighting off the headache blowing up in her skull.

What on Earth am I going to do?

She lifted the trash bin lid to throw away the stick but thought better of it and tucked it into her pocket. She'd take it to her locker and hide it away and put it somewhere safe at home. She already knew without a shadow of a doubt that she wasn't getting rid of her baby, no matter what. Dr. O'Grady didn't even need to know about it—if he didn't have the time.

But how was she going to survive financially? She literally relied on shift work to survive. Putting her palm to her flat belly, she took a deep breath. She'd work it out. Even if it meant selling the house she loved and moving in with her parents. A child had been her dream for far longer than a mortgage had been. So, she'd find a way to do it all, even on her own.

Somehow.

Tabitha pushed through the rest of her shift that day, and the day after that, and the day after that in a blur of fatigue and raw emotion. She was just grateful that her duties as a nurse was so innately ingrained into her, after years of practice, that she made no mistakes when her mind distracted her with thoughts of pregnancy, birthing options, and an eventual baby that would grow up one day to call her 'mom'.

With the countdown to Christmas only three days away, she filled her time when not working with cooking, decorating, and calls with her sister. Not to mention an inordinate amount of gift wrapping. She'd bought all her family small presents throughout the year when she could afford it, and then yesterday she'd gone out and bought even more of everything. She needed the distraction.

Her brother-in-law's money had paid for most of the

Christmas Day festivities, so she blew the rest of the money on presents. A lovely, luxurious coat for her mother, and a stunning new necklace for her sister. On top of that, she practically bought out the pharmacy on pre-natal vitamins and even investigated the housing market. She loved her house, but she couldn't afford it, *and* a baby—and something had to give.

And at night... when there was nothing else to do is when she did her crying. She'd really screwed things up with Noah. And when she thought about it, it had probably been early implantation hormones that had made her so emotional and crotchety. He'd been the first decent guy she'd met, ever, really.

If she looked at the differences between him and her ex-husband, they were simply worlds apart. Even at the start of their relationship with her Ex, when he'd been on his best behavior, there had never been the same comradery, the same attraction, the same... *anything*, really. They'd been doomed from the start, and she'd had blinkers on. But now, she knew better. She knew how much a genuine man who you could connect with was worth.

But how do I make it up to him? Is it even possible?

How could she apologize for being so stupid? So selfish? So... she didn't even have a word for the kind of woman who would ask a man who saved baby's lives, to reduce his hours to suit *her*. Was she mad?

What sort of person does that?

Especially when his lovemaking and every other small gesture of kindness had shown her how caring he was. She continued to formulate a plan, although the catch twenty-two was what was stopping her from simply calling him up and telling him the truth? Because how was he ever going to believe her when she said she wanted him back, if she also told him she was pregnant?

He'd think she trapped him—on purpose. Or worse, he'd think she was only with him for the sake of the baby, and that was the last thing in the world she wanted. Their baby wasn't why she wanted to be with him, but the little life growing inside her had certainly acted as a kick in the pant and a much-needed wake-up call.

She went to sleep on Christmas Eve with an ache in her heart and her hand on her belly.

CHAPTER 18

TABITHA

Christmas Day.

Tabitha was up at the crack of dawn, cleaning and cutting up vegetables and putting the turkey on with all the trimmings. By the time her sister and her mother had arrived, she'd managed to eat a few dry crackers, vomited a dozen times, and polished off two-quart bottles of water. She'd just ticked over seven weeks, and the morning sickness had started.

Perfect timing.

The smell of the roasting turkey made her stomach churn and she blanched. She didn't know how the hell she was supposed to survive this joyous day of feasting when she could scarcely keep anything down.

"Oh, my God! You've done such a good job!" her sister exclaimed as she waddled into Tabitha's kitchen, looking around at the festive table, decorated in a modern silver and blue this year.

"Not as nice as you would have done it, Sam, but I tried." She pulled her sister in for a hug, holding her a little too long, as if she could draw strength from her heavily pregnant little sister.

Sam pulled back with a worried look on her face. "Are you okay?" she asked, ever the discerning one.

Tabitha blinked back the tears that threatened to spill. "Of course. Why wouldn't I be?" she answered quickly, before turning to her mother. "Mom!" She grabbed her mother up for a hug, and kissed the men who'd accompanied her favorite women.

"When did Aunt Theresa say they'd be here?" Mom asked with a smile.

Tabitha glanced at the clock. "About an hour or so, I believe. We've got time to open presents or have a drink. Whatever you guys want." She'd prepared everything just so her mom and sister could relax on their favorite festive day.

"Let's open a few presents, then," said their mom. "I've just got to put the sweet potatoes on to boil." Her mom moved away to grab a saucepan and get started. You really couldn't keep that woman from contributing, even when you tried!

Sam groaned loudly, gasping as she grabbed hold of her husband.

"What's wrong?" Tabitha asked, her heart instantly thumping in her chest at the worrisome sound.

"Um... it's nothing. Just some cramps. They've been going all morning. My silly babies are in the mood to give me a hard time it seems," Sam said through a forced smile.

"All morning? Sam! You're in labor."

She shook her head in absolute denial. "No, I'm not."

A laugh bubbled up inside Tabitha's throat as her heart relaxed. "You're not, huh? Why? Because you don't want to be, Sis?"

Her sister's brow furrowed as she grabbed for her belly again.

The nurse in Tabitha stepped forward, ready for the spotlight. "Hey, John, can you take my sister to my bedroom for a minute? Lie her down on the bed for me."

"Why?" Sam asked as John directed his wife down the hall.

"I'll be there in a minute," Tabitha called back as they disappeared from sight. Tabitha grinned at her mom. "I'm going to go check out Sam, because I'm pretty sure she's in labor."

Their mother smiled with glee and clapped her hands with grandmotherly excitement. "Oh, goodness! I hope everything's going to be okay with her and the babies."

"Oh, I'm sure they'll all be fine. She has a brilliant obstetrician."

Her mom stepped forward and opened her mouth, as though to ask a question.

"Hold that thought," said Tabitha. "I'll be right back."

Darn Sam!

Of course, she had told their mother about Tabitha's dates with the handsome doctor. She never could keep anything a secret, even when they were little kids. She was utterly hopeless when it came to surprises.

Tabitha grabbed a sheet from the linen closet and walked into her room.

"Tabitha, what are we doing in here?" Sam asked, her tone one of annoyance.

Wow, she really doesn't want to have these babies today!

She smiled patiently, swallowing her chuckle. "Just lie on your back, Sam."

"But, I..."

"Just do as you're told, for once. John, can you go keep Dad company for me?"

John backed toward the door and left with a nod, happy to leave the women to it.

Meanwhile, Tabitha wrangled her sister, who had luckily worn a long winter skirt. "I need your panties off, Sis, can you do it... or do you need my help?"

Sam groaned, her cheeks flushing with color. "Help, please."

Tabitha pulled her up to a stand, then kneeled and quickly pulled her sister's underwear off. Then she encouraged Sam to lie down on the bed and bend her knees. "Now, just relax, I'm going to check your cervix for dilation."

"Why?" her sister groaned at her.

"Because I really think you're already in labor, and if you are, we probably need to get you to the hospital. If you're not, then we can relax and enjoy Christmas without fuss."

"I just want to enjoy Christmas," Sam whined with an openly pouty expression.

Tabitha shook her head as she pulled on a rubber glove she'd grabbed from the bathroom and slid her fingers in to check her sister's cervix. She almost couldn't look as the two sides of her personality warred against each other. The sister part just ridiculously just screamed *"Ew!"* while her nurse personality was efficient in her job and nonplussed.

Four centimeters already.

She withdrew her hand and tapped her sister's thigh with a grin. "Let's get you something to eat."

Sam grinned at her. "Oh great, that means I'm not in labor, right?"

Tabitha helped her sister get to her feet and they walked back to the kitchen. "Quite the opposite, Sam. You're very much in labor and will probably deliver tonight, but you may as well enjoy my turkey before you go in."

Sam's eyes widened comically, and her mouth opened and closed like a fish gulping above water.

Tabitha did a little dance of joy as she grabbed her sister's hands in her own. "I can't believe you ignored the signs all morning, Sis. You're going to have your babies very soon. You're going to be a mom!"

There was a general squeal of excitement in the room as Sam bent over to groan and gasp once again, clearly not quite as thrilled as the rest of us as she rode the waves of her early contractions.

Today was going to be a very special day for them all—forever. Their family was about to grow by two amazing little members, and a jolt of infectious glee filled her at the thought.

I'm going to be an aunt! Without even needing to think about it, she resolved to be the best damn aunt there ever was. She'd love those little tykes to death and spoil them rotten, and there wasn't a damn thing Sam could do about it! Aunties, like grandparents, got a free pass, after all. It was going to be all sugar, treats, and cuddles for days.

Her own troubles forgotten, she grinned to herself.

This is going to be the best Christmas ever!

CHAPTER 19

NOAH

Christmas lunch at his parents' home was even nicer than he remembered. The addition of his nieces and nephews meant that his folks really went all-out on the decorations, food, and the tree; which was probably the most magnificent one he'd ever seen in real life. It was covered in flashing lights, sparkling tinsel, and more baubles than you could count and atop its tip balanced a glorious golden star.

"We're so glad you could make it this year," his dad said as they sat on the back deck with a hot drink in hand.

The snow was falling which was a bit unusual for Seattle during Christmas, but it was certainly beautiful. It covered the backyard in a picturesque dusting of white, like icing sugar on a cake.

"Yeah, it's been too long," Noah agreed, because it really had been.

"Well, work always came first, and we understood that, Son. Your mother and I are very proud of you and all that you've accomplished. You've made a lot of sacrifices to get where you are today."

Noah took a long drink of his eggnog thoughtfully. It seemed the season brought out the best in everyone. His father rarely offered such praise so directly. It was nice and made him feel that his efforts hadn't gone unnoticed by those he cared about most. Although, now, surrounded by his ever-growing family, Noah was the one who was proud. They had a truly beautiful family unit, and he was glad to be a part of it.

"Thanks, Dad, but I've been trying to make a few changes regarding that recently," he admitted.

"Yeah? Would that have something to do with a certain young lady named Tabitha?"

Noah glanced over at his father. "What do you mean?"

"I mean... she was here, and now she's not and you haven't mentioned her. So, I'm assuming things didn't go quite the way you had planned."

Am I really that transparent?

"Yeah, well, she made a point or two that I took into consideration, and I've since added another physician to my practice. A young doctor, willing to learn what I know, and fill in for me when I need him to. And most importantly, he's enthusiastic about doing things my way, to my standard of care and professionalism. With two of us in the practice, it can expand a bit, and we'll both have coverage for holidays and vacations."

"Is that why you're here today?"

Noah nodded. "Yes. Although I may need to go in tomorrow, my partner has Christmas covered."

It had been a good suggestion of Tabitha's, there was no denying it, although at the time he'd struggled to hear anything other than her condemnation.

"That's great, Noah. Hopefully it'll free you up a little to have more time off so that you can live a life beyond the workplace now, after all these years."

"Yeah, that's the hope, Dad."

And perhaps more time to date or to mend bridges with Tabitha.

Because he really felt that deep down, beyond his initial hurt, that she was definitely someone worth pursuing—worth loving. And where no one else had reached him, she'd made him realize the value of his time—and the time he lost. You were supposed to work to live, right? Not live to work...

She also fit into his family so well, and he felt the lack of her today, more than any other time over the past three weeks. And that was strange. To be happily surrounded by his big, crazy family, who loved him more than anyone on the planet, and *still* feel her absence? That said something about what they shared, and more than anything he wished Tabitha could be there with him. To share this day with him; a day he'd told her quite flippantly that he'd rather work through then stop and enjoy. He pulled his coat tighter around himself and let his head fall back against the house with a sigh.

Damn. I fucked this up really good.

Nothing short of a Christmas miracle would likely see him having another chance with Tabitha to make things right. Two seconds later his phone began to ring in his pocket. It was the hospital. "Shit. I'm sorry, Dad. I told them not to call me."

"Hey, you made it through lunch *and* presents. No one's going to hold it against you if you have to leave now," his father assured him.

He smiled his thanks at his dad for his understanding as he answered the phone. "Dr. O'Grady."

"I'm sorry to disturb you, Dr. O'Grady."

Noah sat up in his chair straighter, his attention grabbed immediately. It was his new partner and co-physician, Dr. Smith. "Dr. Smith, what's wrong?" he asked. If he was calling, it was because he was facing something he couldn't handle. "Nothing yet, but the staff have just received a phone call from a Tabitha Jones and she's relayed that her sister is currently in natural labor with twins—one of which is breach. I'm sorry, but I'm not comfortable attempting a natural labor with a multiple birth. If she wants a C-section I can..."

Noah's heart pounded in his chest.

Samantha.

"No, no. She's quite set on trying for a natural labor, so I'll come in now. Did Tabitha happen to say how dilated she was?" Knowing Tabitha, she would be checking.

"About six centimeters at last check," Dr. Smith confirmed.

"That's great. She's well on her way. I'll see you in about half an hour. This is one you'll want to stick around for."

"We'll keep her as comfortable as we can until you arrive," Dr. Smith acknowledged.

They hung up and Noah offered his apologies to his family before he ran out the door at breakneck speed, his heart pounding in his ears all the way. It was like the Christmas miracle he'd secretly been hoping for and for someone who wasn't normally a fan of the holiday in question, that statement said *a lot*. He'd be seeing Tabitha a lot sooner than he'd dared hope for.

I just hope I can fix this.

CHAPTER 20

TABITHA

"Just breathe, Sam. That's all you need to do at the moment. Breathe, and don't let the panic consume you. Focus on riding the waves, let them carry you away. Don't fight them," Tabitha coached.

Sam squeezed her hand tighter as she blew out a steady stream of deep breaths. Her younger sister hadn't let go of her hand in almost two hours, and it was getting more numb with every passing moment. But she wouldn't deprive Sam of one of the few comforts a woman could rely on during a tough natural birth. The simple relief of connection—of having someone there for you as you endured a rite of passage which you had absolutely no control over.

They'd finally arrived at the hospital after what seemed like an eternity. John had been forced to drive his precious cargo slower than usual because of the wintery road conditions

"Okay," Tabitha said when they pulled into the emergency bay. "You go in with John and I'll bring your bags along."

"No!" Sam panicked, her eyes wide and her heart in her throat. "I want you."

"Argh... all right. But you need to let up on my hand a bit, I'm losing feeling over here."

Sam let go in an instant. She was clearly willing to do whatever it took to keep her experienced nurse sister by her side.

Tabitha gasped at the throbbing pain the blood restoration brought and grimaced as she gave her fingers a quick rub to regain feeling properly. "Okay, stay put. I'm just going to get a wheelchair and then we'll all go inside, together, okay?"

Sam nodded. "Thank you," she breathed, very obviously relieved with this course of action over the original plan.

Tabitha jumped out of the car and met the ER staff at the double doors that led into the Emergency Department as they wheeled a chair out.

It took just a few minutes to get Sam safely into the chair and into an examination room, but by the time they did, Samantha's skirts were soaked, and she was frantically yelling.

"I think I just wet myself!" she half-shrieked, her voice shrill, and her expression absolutely mortified.

Tabitha couldn't stop laughing, the absurdity of the situation bubbling inside her like a pot of oil put on to boil. Hadn't her sister done her research?

Surely, she knew about the various stages of birthing...

She'd always just assumed by Sam's carefree attitude that she'd read up all that she needed to for a twin delivery and felt confident about what was to come. "Sis, calm down. It's okay and very normal. Your water has broken, which is a good thing. It means everything is progressing, and your body is doing exactly what it needs to, to make sure your beautiful babies will be here soon."

"Listen to her, she knows what she's talking about." A familiar voice announced as it burst into the room.

Tabitha swung around, her heart in her throat as every nerve in her body instantly ignited with recognition and memory. "Noah!"

He smiled at her in the way she'd been dreaming about... like he missed her, and didn't hate her at all, as she'd feared.

"Tabitha. I see you've brought me my patient. Are you staying for the birth?"

Tabitha's heart sunk from her throat and back into her chest to thump away like a drum. All the while heat raced to her cheeks and her belly at the sight of her handsome doctor. "That wasn't the original plan, but..."

"She's not going anywhere! I need her," Sam insisted from behind them, her gaze intense with conviction.

Tabitha somehow managed to drag her eyes away from Noah's handsome face to attend to her sister.

"I'll stay if you want me to, hon. But what about John?"

John came running into the room a moment later with three bags and a bundle of nervous energy that was like a rock tossed into their pool of calm.

"What about John?" he repeated, looking between them all.

"Um... my sister wants me to stay for the birth. Are you okay with that?" Tabitha asked. She'd assumed he'd want to be present for the birth, but not all men had the constitution to deal with the nitty gritty of it when it came down to it.

He nodded rapidly and set down the bags. "Of course, I am," he answered without even a second's hesitation. "Whatever she wants is fine by me."

Tabitha caught Noah looking at John with a surprised expression and she grinned. "Yeah, my sister chose well. Didn't she?"

Noah nodded. "I think so. Noah O'Grady," he said, extending his hand and introducing himself to John.

Tabitha felt the need to add something as she watched them. Maybe Sam's husband's nervous energy was infectious. "John works too much too, you know, so you two have a lot in common, actually. The only difference is that Sam is super supportive of his choices too, and I'm... not. Not yet," she trailed off, mentally imploring the doctor to understand what she was so desperately trying to say.

Noah came forward and started to say something but was cut off.

"Seriously? Now? Can't you two just leave your shit alone for two minutes? I need some help over here! *Please*." Sam screamed out from the examination bed.

Tabitha grimaced in shame, having been derailed by the presence of the father of her own secret baby, and rushed to be near to her sister "All right, Samantha, back to business. Let's see how far along you are."

Noah moved into action and began his examination, checking on dilation and effacement of her cervix.

Tabitha concentrated solely on her sister for the next three hours. Her own baby dramas could wait. Right now, her little sis needed her full attention.

Sam was everything you'd expect a pregnant woman could be. Loud and angry, tired and serene, powerful and seemingly helpless all at once.

Perfect, in every way.

Through a long, sweat-drench labor, her sister showed her what true strength was. She growled her way through each brutal contraction and shuddered with the monstrous effort of a twin delivery. Then, at eleven o'clock at night, her beautiful, strong sister pushed two amazingly perfect babies into the world. One little boy and one little girl. Both were small, as was to be expected with multiple-fetus pregnancies, but screamingly healthy and pink as cotton candy.

"Oh my God. They're so beautiful," Tabitha breathed. Her heart had never felt so full as when she gazed down at her sister. Naked, sweaty, bloody, and her arms full of the squirming vernix-covered flesh of her two infant children.

"Noah, thank you so much," Sam sobbed, tears of absolute and undeniable bliss streaking her flushed cheeks. "Everyone said a natural delivery with twins wasn't possible but look at us!"

Noah nodded and then stepped away and smiled as he pulled off his gloves.

"How about we leave the new family to bond. The nurses will help you with anything else you need, Sam. Congratulations to you both. You'll make wonderful parents."

Tabitha followed the doctor's cue and dragged herself away from her new family in order to let John step in and kiss his wife and adore the babies he'd helped create. When they made it into the hallway Tabitha threw herself at Noah for the tightest hug imaginable. "Thank you *so* much for everything you just did in there for my sister."

She knew the statistics on births, especially multiple births, and what Noah had just achieved with her sister was nothing short of miraculous. Between his careful intervention and manipulation, along with his calm, positive coaching, he'd guided Sam to victory; and helped her experience the birth she'd dreamed of.

Noah squeezed her back, his embrace firm and familiar.

She sagged against him. God she'd missed the smell of him, his warmth, and the sound of his laugh.

"Merry Christmas, Tabitha."

She pulled back and smiled at him. "Merry Christmas, Noah," he answered before she took a deep breath. "There is so much I need to tell you—to apologize for... but I don't know if this is the best time." She glanced hesitantly around at the staff in the hallway.

"How about we talk in my office?" he offered. Noah took her hand and led her into his office. The place where they'd first met.

Her hand tingled where he touched her and the butterflies in her stomach had once again taken wing. "It was so good of you to come in for Sam. The doctor on rotation told us that you had Christmas off," she began, the words tumbling out of her. The fact Noah had been off work had surprised the hell out of her, and in her panic, she'd asked the man to call him in. "I'm really sorry if we pulled you away from your family."

They sat down in the two patients chairs beside his desk, facing each other, still holding hands. The fact that Noah didn't seem to want to let her go was a great sign and boded well for them. It helped to push aside some of the fears that had consumed her the past few weeks.

"No... I was glad you called. I wouldn't have missed it for the world."

"You're such a good doctor," Tabitha whispered. "And I'm so sorry for the things I said that day on the phone. I've been ashamed of myself ever since to be honest." She dropped her head and focused on his skilled hands, still slightly white from the powdered latex gloves.

"No, stop, please. You don't need to be sorry. I'm the one who didn't listen to you or communicate the way I should have, Tabitha. After all these years of training, you'd think I'd be better at talking to women." He smiled at his own joke.

Tabitha couldn't stop herself from reaching out to cup his jaw, her eyes glistening with tears that threatened to spill. "Can we start again?" she asked hopefully with bated breath. "I mean... will you forgive me for being so ungrateful, so thoughtless..."

Noah silenced her, pressing his lips to hers softly and passionately, until she couldn't think about anything other than gripping his scrub top and pulling him in tightly to her.

But as it was want to do, the door opened and a voice called in. "Dr. O'Grady, we need you."

Tabitha pulled away and smiled up at the regretful look in Noah's beautiful eyes.

"I'm sorry I—" he began.

But Tabitha only grinned, her heart near to bursting with joy. "Oh, trust me, after that miraculous birth I just witnessed? I'd say you have a pass to run out on me in any situation for the next decade or so. Go."

Noah laughed, his endearing, hearty laugh that she'd missed so much. "Thank you, Tabitha. I'll get in touch when I can." He kissed her quickly, in front of the other doctor, and ran back to attend to his patients like the real, modern-day superhero he was.

I can't believe it...

Tabitha pressed her fingertips to her lips, absorbing the heat of his mouth and sighing at the Christmas magic that had truly been performed today. With her heart and mind on Cloud Nine, she wandered back to her sister's room for hugs and goodbyes, and then called an uber. It was after midnight and it was a new day, and a whole new world.

But there was just one more, tiny little thing she needed to take care of.

CHAPTER 21

NOAH

"Dr. O'Grady, your next patient is here," said his personal receptionist.

Noah lifted his head from his notes, his brow momentarily furrowed. He hadn't been expecting anyone for another hour. "All right. Show them in."

Tabitha stuck her head in and waved. and

Happiness struck his heart like an arrow from Cupid's bow.

God she's beautiful.

"I hope I'm not disturbing you," she said as she stepped into the room, her face shining with a health he couldn't explain.

Christmas had obviously done her a world of good. "I was just popping by to see my sister and thought I'd say 'hi'."

He rose from his leather chair and walked around his desk, taking her in his arms and kissing her.

She didn't fight him, quite the opposite in fact. She came into his arms willingly with a smile and kissed him with an answering moan on her lips.

They were back on track, and it made his soul sing. "Your sister's doing great," he told her. "They can all go home in two or three days. The twins have been putting weight on like little champions."

Tabitha smiled and the light reached her eyes. "Thanks for looking after them so well."

Noah shrugged, holding her close. "It's my job," he said simply. Her warmth made him crave home, his bed, and sleep. She was his comfort and he'd missed her more than he'd realized.

"Who was the physician who was working here yesterday? A floater?" she asked inquisitively.

"Ah, sort of." He drew her down to sit on the patient's chairs, as he had the night before. He'd put a few things into action since their break-up phone call and he just hoped she'd be happy with the changes. He'd meant it when he'd said he'd move mountains for her. "He's my new partner. I made him an offer two weeks ago and he accepted."

"Your new partner?" she asked as her eyebrows rose, and he could see the cogs ticking away behind her clever eyes.

"Yes, it was your suggestion, after all," he reminded her.

"My suggestion? You mean you..." she trailed off.

He waited patiently for her to finish, but instead her breathing rate had increased, and she wasn't speaking at all. She was simply staring at him, speechless. "Please, continue," he prompted after a time.

She swallowed hard, her throat working up and down. "Um...

you mean you really added another doctor to do alternate shifts for you?"

"Yes," he answered truthfully, enjoying the strange mix of emotions flittering across her lovely face.

"Ah... but why?" She glanced down at her feet and then up into his eyes again.

He grinned, letting the happiness he'd been waiting for—for three weeks now—to fill up his chest. He'd made these changes *for her*, and he wanted her to know it. "So that I could have a life..." he admitted softly. "With you, if you'd still like that?"

Tabitha's mouth fell open and she covered her mouth in genuine surprise. "Oh, my God. Yes, Noah, I do. I very much still do!" She reached over and grabbed his hands. "I thought you'd never forgive me for wanting you to change your work. I know how much it means to you. It's not just your career, it's your life's passion. Your reason."

He shook his head, pursing his lips. Looking back, now, he saw how frustrating it all must have been for her. But hindsight was always twenty-twenty, and he'd sorely needed the wake-up call. "No, you were right to complain. But I can't guarantee I'll never have run off in the middle of a date again—"

"Oh, I don't expect..." she interrupted, but forged ahead.

"But this makes everything much easier, you were right about that. We can go on short vacations and I can have nights off and not be on call. It may take a year or so to get him up to speed with the way I do things, for instance, birthing twins naturally. Though, he's young, bright, and I'm confident he'll learn quickly."

Tabitha smiled brightly at his reasoning and nodded, her breath catching in an unusual way.

"But long-term, I think this will be great. For me, my patients... and us," he finished.

She tightened her grip on his hand. "So... you really want to get back together?" she asked.

He nodded, a smile tugging at the edges of his lips. "Yes. Very much. I've missed you more than I can ever describe, Tabitha and I don't want to lose you again."

She looked down again at her feet, her gaze lingering there for longer than was comfortable.

Worry gripped his heart and his mind raced for an explanation.

Am I too late to try to fix this?

No, it couldn't be that. Her kisses had revealed just much she'd missed him too. She'd seemed entirely genuine. Or was he mistaken? Was he reading into this all wrong?

"What is it, Tabitha? What's wrong?" he pressed, unable to hold back the niggling doubts bubbling to the surface.

"Um... it's nothing. Do you have time to chat for a bit longer?"

Noah glanced at the door, once again feeling the odd tug-of-war that came with dealing with his personal life and his business life. "I'd love to, but Cheryl said I had another patient. Maybe I should let her know we need a bit longer?" He pushed his chair out to stand up.

Tabitha laughed. "No... No. Your next patient is *me*."

"Oh... was that how you managed to get in to see me? You don't need to do that, Tabby," he said with a grin and a shake of his head. How adorable was she? Gaming the system like that.

"Um, no. I mean, um... I need an obstetrician and I was hoping you could fit me into your schedule," she explained, her expression plaintive and hopeful.

"What?"

I couldn't have possibly heard that correctly.

"I... I'm pregnant, Noah."

"How?" he breathed, his entire world on the brink of implosion. "I don't understand. How?" he repeated.

She laughed nervously, pulling her hands away to wring her fingers in her lap. "Well, to be honest I haven't had the pregnancy confirmed but I've done a stick test, had no period for seven full weeks now, and have been fairly sick every morning for about a week or so..." she trailed off, leaving the rest unsaid.

"Oh my God." He had *no* idea what to say. He hadn't been expecting anything like this! Not that it was unwelcome news, but...

"Are you angry?" she asked quickly. "Because honestly, this wasn't planned at all, and I would never, ever want to trap you. So, I don't want you to feel like I did this on purpose, or that you *have* to be with me because of it. ...But I had to be honest with you. You deserve the truth. You are a baby doctor, after all."

Noah reached across the space between them and pulled her onto his lap, his heart no longer on the verge of implosion. Instead, his entire world had just exploded in the most incredible and miraculous way imaginable. Planned or not, he'd always wanted a family and of all people, he knew damn well babies did their own thing on their own time. "Come here, you beautiful girl."

She came and shuddered a little against him, as though she were suppressing tears.

"I can't imagine how scared you've been, or what you've gone through the last few weeks, Tabitha. I'm so sorry." He'd dealt with enough single mothers firsthand to know how terrifying the prospect of raising a child alone could be.

"No... no. I... um..." she stammered. She couldn't seem to get the words out.

So, alleviating her of the need to do so, he simply put his arms around her and shushed her, soothing away all her fears and anxieties the best way he knew how. "You don't need to explain anything. But how about we get the ultrasound machine out and have a look at our baby, what do you think about that?" he asked.

Her head popped up from where it had rested on his shoulder. "Seriously?"

"Of course. I can't let you hire me as your obstetrician, obviously. But as the mother of my child, we can share this special first moment together."

She nodded and grabbed a tissue off my desk and dabbed at her glistening eyes.

"Come, lie down." He directed her to the table he'd seen thousands of patients on before. But this time his breath shuddered in his throat as he pulled over the machine and got the equipment ready, just as he had a thousand times before.

"Are you okay?" she asked him, her brows creased with concern.

An unexpected and surprised laugh burst from his throat. "This is the first time I'm going to see a child of mine on this machine... and it's just ... *surreal.*"

She smiled as she pulled up her top.

He applied some clear gel and placed the probe low on her belly. At seven weeks it would be safer to do an internal ultrasound, but if he was lucky, he should be able to see something. "There! Look." He froze the image and there before them, like a still from a dream, was a little white jellybean with a rapid heart rate beating away wildly.

"That's the baby," Tabitha whispered into the room, her eyes glued to the screen. The tears she'd so valiantly tried to wipe and hide streamed down her cheeks in plain sight and it was the most beautiful thing he'd ever seen.

He turned and bent to kiss her soft lips. "That's *our* baby," he corrected gently, a broad grin lighting up his whole expression. And then a deep sense of comfort and peace fell over his office unlike any he had ever felt in his life. And with that kiss, and those few spoken words between them, they began their new lives together—soon to be a family of three.

EPILOGUE

NOAH

Christmas the following year...

Noah juggled the diaper bag in one hand and a picnic basket full of Christmas goodies in the other. The trunk was full to overflowing with gifts for his family, and there was no way he was going to be able to do it all in one trip. He rounded the car and put his hand in the small of Tabitha's back. It was beginning to snow—the powdered ice falling from the sky in perfect crystals—and he didn't want either of his girls to get cold.

"I'll come back for the presents once you're settled and warm, let's just get you both inside," he said to his gorgeous new wife.

Tabitha held their baby daughter in her arms protectively as the breeze picked up. "Okay, thank you, hon."

It was Christmas morning and they'd promised his mom they'd be at her house early. So, with their minds on the clock they'd eaten a quick breakfast, got ready, packed up the car, and had arrived with time to spare.

"Be careful of the ice," Tabitha warned him, as she pulled the woolen blanket more tightly around their precious bundle as they hurried together toward the enormous and spectacularly decorated house.

They got under shelter of the porch and Noah reached out and opened the door. It was unlocked, as expected, and a burst of warmth and raucous sound washed over them through the door in stark contrast to the weather behind them. "Hey, Mom! We're here." he called out.

His mother ran toward them with her arms outstretched. And it wasn't to hold or embrace *him*. "How's my perfect baby grand-daughter," she cooed, reaching for their baby and scooping her up out of Tabitha's arms.

"She slept a little more soundly last night," Tabitha enlightened her with a sigh of exhaustion. His poor wife had been woken mercilessly every two hours for most of the night.

"Come in, come in," Mom said, finally leaning forward to kiss us both before ushering us inside. "Merry Christmas."

"Merry Christmas, Mom."

My mother grinned like the old salt she was when it came to grandchildren and hurried off with our baby.

Tabitha and Noah exchanged rueful looks. It was great that his mom adored Sienna so much, but truthfully, they were still getting used to the fact that everyone else treated their baby like she was theirs. She was forever being scooped up, carted off, and cuddled to within an inch of her life. Perhaps if they weren't so damn tired, they'd likely have found more humor in the situation, but they were still definitely in early parent panic mode. Despite their best efforts to chill out, they found themselves watching the baby like a pair of hawks most of the time.

Tabitha yawned and leaned against me, her warmth and familiar perfume overcoming my senses. "I still can't believe you're really here, Noah."

Noah lifted her chin and kissed her lips. "I wouldn't have missed our baby's first Christmas for the world. You girls *are* my world."

Tabitha sighed against his lips, and they shared one perfect blissful moment, before his nieces and nephews came charging at them, and the whirlwind of Christmas festivity took over.

There was shimmering glitter and tinsel from one end of the house to the other, as well as spent party poppers, unraveled streamers, and shredded wrapping paper in all the colors of the rainbow galore. His mother's home looked like poor old Santa had thrown up his festive cheer all over the place—and it was undeniably glorious. It was officially their first Christmas as a complete family; all their parents' children *and* theirs, together for one splendid, memory saturated day.

The cheerful atmosphere, the delicious food and drink, as well as the constant shrieking and laughter of the kids filled Noah with a feeling he didn't think he'd ever experienced before. And then the realization struck him like a bolt of lightning from the heavens that for the first time since he was a child himself, this felt like *home*. A chaotic, noisy, love-filled home.

He just wished his work anxieties would calm the fuck down for a bit so he could properly enjoy it. That was something he was still getting used to, especially with the idea of Christmas miracle babies on his mind. A part of him kept trying to convince him that he should be at the hospital 'just in case', but he squashed the inner voice down as best he could.

It wasn't until hours later, when he was sitting with his brothers and having a whiskey, that he finally began to really feel more relaxed. They hadn't been interrupted and it was bliss.

Sienna was fast asleep in her mother's arms, while Tabitha was happily being spoon-fed desserts and drinks, within the protective and accepting circle of her new family.

"You know," his dad said. "I don't remember the last Christmas you came here and actually managed to stay through all three courses."

Noah grimaced and took another sip of his whiskey and sighed, enjoying the burn as it ran down his throat. "Yeah, me neither," he admitted.

"Are you on call?" one of his brothers asked, as though he couldn't quite believe Noah was still there either. "I mean... are you going in later?"

Noah shook his head. "No. I've actually taken this whole week off." Silence descended all around him and as he stared at his father, whose mouth was practically hanging open.

"What?" Noah asked with a chuckle. "Is that really *so* amazing?"

Another brother guffawed and practically choked on his bourbon. "Ah yeah, it *really* is..."

Noah swallowed hard. This past year had been a true challenge for him. He'd promised Tabitha he'd be there for her, and he had been. He kept his promises no matter how hard they were to keep. But old habits died hard and he found himself doing extra hours and shifts on occasion in an attempt to satiate that niggling, burning need to *do more*.

"Was I really that bad?" Noah asked him, wanting the truth even if it hurt, because sometimes, it was the only thing that worked to bring him back to reality—to the world beyond his career and the hospital.

"Ah, well... it's not that you were ever bad, son," his dad said, though his face hinted at another story.

"It's okay," Noah assured him. "You can be honest with me."

"Well," his dad began, leaning back in his chair, a cold beer in hand, despite the fact it was snowing outside. "You know we're all very proud of you, you're a good doctor, and a good man. But there's more to life than work, my boy. And for the longest time, that was all you had. Your mother and I were afraid that you'd never get to see or enjoy of the rest of what life has to offer."

"Yeah," his elder brother laughed. "You were missing out! Diapers, and sleepless nights, and a wife that's at you for something or another, twenty-four-seven." He chortled, then winked to show that he was joking.

Noah just smiled. He loved his life now. Was it often harder? Definitely yes. How about more challenging? That was an affirmative. Even uncontrollable sometimes? Absolutely! But he couldn't imagine changing any of it—not a single thing—even if he could.

"Speaking of which, I better go check on the old ball and chain," he said, grinning at his brother, who'd already been married a decade longer than him. Noah shook his hand and smiled. "Merry Christmas."

"I'm glad you're here, Noah," he said, in a rare moment of seriousness.

"Me too," Noah agreed, and left the men's circle to go and sit with his beautiful girls. the two incredible females who comprised his whole world.

"Everything okay?" Tabitha asked when he came to sit down. "Has the office called? Or..."

Noah shook his head. "Nope. We're all good, beautiful. I've told Mick and Terry that the only reason they're allowed to call me this week is if one of them breaks an arm. And a broken leg isn't good enough! They can still bloody well work with a moon boot on."

Everyone around us laughed and Tabitha shifted closer to him, leaning into his side.

Noah had been forced to hire another associate a few months ago to cover his leave when Tabitha had given birth. Despite trying for a natural labor, she'd ended up needing a C-section. And with such major, albeit common, abdominal surgery, she'd needed him at home to care for the baby while she healed.

That time had been priceless, and he'd never regret those days. Bathing his precious newborn baby and holding her as she slept... it had been the most incredible bonding time. And now, more than ever, he didn't understand why more fathers didn't appreciate being hands-on carers for their own offspring. Caring for Sienna was a dream come true.

So, after Tabitha had fully recovered and been able and willing to take over full time care of their baby, Noah realized that he didn't in fact want to go back to work full time ever again. He'd asked Dr. Terry Smith to stay on, and now there were three of them to treat patients, and they all managed to enjoy a life outside the cool, white walls of the hospital as well.

There was no denying he was still busy, and there were always those dates he missed, and the occasional family birthday party he had to leave early. But those days were few and far between the more time passed, and Tabitha forgave me those moments because when she really needed him, he was there.

I always would be.

And that was the most important thing in the world to him, ultimately. That his patient, gorgeous, and nurturing wife felt loved and appreciated, because she truly was. She had made his life whole. It was her and her alone that reached him through his workaholic haze. She taught him that there was more to life, and he'd never forget it or stop being grateful for her determination and will to dare ask for something better, because he'd needed it too. He just hadn't been able to see it at the time.

"Merry Christmas Noah," Tabitha whispered to him, turning her face up for a kiss, her eyes brimming with peace and love.

Noah smiled and pressed his lips to hers, relishing in her need to be touched, to be soothed, to be reminded she wasn't alone in this—and that she never would be.

Tabitha, my wife and the mother of my child.

His heart swelled. She was the woman he was going to spend the rest of his life adoring. Because of her, they had a life worth envying, a life overflowing with everything good, wholesome, and sometimes... outright sexy. Which reminded him... the second they got Sienna to sleep at home, he was going to seize the opportunity to *show* his wife just how much he needed and desired her.

I can't believe I ever hated Christmas!

THE END.